David Neth

HEAT

BLACK MAGNET

Book 1

DN Publishing

Black Magnet
Heat, Book 1

Batavia, NY

www.DavidNethBooks.com

ISBN: 978-1-945336-64-5
First edition

Subscribe to the author's newsletter for updates and exclusive content:
DavidNethBooks.com/Newsletter

Follow the author at:
www.facebook.com/DavidNethBooks
www.instagram.com/dneth13

Also by David Neth

Heat

Black Magnet

Dust Storm

The Gatekeeper

Fuse

Origin

Omertà

Oblivion

Under the Moon

The Full Moon

The Harvest Moon

The Blood Moon

The Crescent Moon

The Blue Moon

The Art of Magic

Standalone

All I Ever Wanted

Chapter One

Piercing sounds echo in my ears. I'm thrown against a rocky surface. My right side takes the brunt of it. Instantly, my shoulder begins throbbing in pain.

Then, silence.

I groan, my voice sounding foreign to me. My body aches all over, but still I force myself to sit up. I open my eyes, but don't see anything. I shut them tight and reopen them again.

Still nothing.

Everything's dark.

Desperately, I turn my head, searching for any trace of light. Behind me, I spot the tiniest sliver. I follow it.

Once on my feet, my bare right foot slips on the rock below me, but I'm able to catch myself with my left. I'm only wearing one shoe.

The air smells like something burning—or something that has since burned. Like a campfire the following morning. It's further amplified by the layer of grime I can feel all over my body, coating my skin, making it almost slick, just like the rock I'm stepping on. And it's cold in here, too. My fingers and toes—especially the bare ones—are even going numb from the lack of heat.

A low growl grows from deep in the shadows, followed by a chilling breeze. At first, I'm not positive that it's even real, until the sound grows so loud that it feels like the floor is shaking. Then, in an instant, it's gone, along with the wind. The silence echoes in my ears and goosebumps prickle my skin, making me wonder if it even happened.

What the hell is going on?

I need to get out of here. I'm afraid I hear more traces of another growl starting up. The longer I spend in here, the more it gives me the creeps. I don't know if it's just in my head, but I can't help but feel like there's something sinister lying just beyond the surface, hidden in the darkness.

My bare foot jams against a rock as I move closer to the light. My eyes adjust in the darkness and I can just make out the sharp edges of the boulder. Reaching up, I climb on top of it, shifting around a few large rocks to make the small crevice where the light's coming from big enough for even my thin frame to fit through. My body scrapes against the unforgiving surfaces as I pull myself through, but it's better than staying trapped.

The other side is warmer and the light shining from the end of the tunnel is blinding. My eyes burn, even as I turn away from the light. But deeper into the tunnel, past the crevice I just escaped from, I feel a growing sense of unease and danger.

I need to get out of here.

Turning, I take careful steps toward the light, squinting at the harsh sun. Still, the light seems to rekindle my memory. Or rather, my lack of one. I have no idea how I got here or why I'm so disheveled.

Actually, I don't remember much of anything. How I got in this cave, what city I live in, who my parents are—I don't even

Chapter One

know my own name.

No, *that* I do remember. Ashton—Ash. That's who I am.

But that's it. That's all I remember. Not the place I rest my head each night. Not any memories from years ago. Not even a single person who cares about me.

What the hell happened in that cave?

I turn and look back at the crevice I crawled out of, even more dread building up inside of me as I hear another grumble. I need to get out of here.

Luckily, my eyes have adjusted enough for me to pick up my pace. As I move I look around to try to find things to jog my memory. My one bare foot is black from what appears to be soot, as are my arms and the rest of me. My shirt especially is so torn I might as well not even be wearing one. At least I have my pants.

I make it to the end of the tunnel and squint at the light from what appears to be a setting sun. Reluctantly, I have to turn around and face the cave again because my eyes burn too bad. Still not used to this much light. I must've been in that cave for a while, but I can't remember.

When I turn back around, I search for the glowing setting sun, but I can't see it. It must be on the other side of the mountain, meaning I'm facing east. That's a start to figuring out where I am.

I take in the view, instantly stumbling back a step. I'm a hundred feet high, overlooking a dense city that's situated in the valley between two mountain ranges. There's a river that runs through the city, underneath the myriad of streets and buildings. Clustered together, several towers rise high in the sky, challenging the height of the mountains. Nature still wins this battle. Despite the urban environment, a lot of the city is green from trees blooming between structures. Once again, nature wins.

The view is spectacular—and frightening—but I need to get down there somehow. Find someone who might be willing to help me figure out who I am and where I live. Hell, I'd kill for a shower first. And a meal. Not that any bystander on the street is going to give me the time of day in my present state, but anything's better than the cave.

The fresh air passing from outside makes the hair on the back of my neck stand up even more. It's a warm breeze. Completely in contrast to the cold cave.

It appears as though there's an overgrown path along the rocky wall leading down to the city. Or, at least I hope it leads down to the city. Maybe it's an animal path. Maybe it'll lead to a dead-end and I'll have to backtrace my steps. Either way, the inviting warmth from the sun leads me down. I just want to put distance between me and this damned cave. Is that a part of who I am? Claustrophobic? Paranoid? I wonder how quickly I'll remember who I am.

Kicking back weeds, ducking under thick tree branches, I keep a look out for any insects or animals I might accidentally step on with my exposed foot. Add a fear of snakes to the growing list of things I'm learning about myself.

My hand trails along the rocky wall until the path curls around in the opposite direction, snaking its way down the mountain. I try to remember as much as I can, but my mind is blank. Nothing's up there. The light's on but nobody's home. Well, as far as my memory goes.

I don't remember anything. Nothing besides my name, that is. It's a wonder I even remember that. Must be it's ingrained in my head so much that it's impossible to forget. But that begs the question: does that mean there's no one in my life that's so ingrained in my memory that I can't remember them?

The sun's rays dwindle over the course of the hour it takes me to walk down. My mouth is bone dry. I need nourishment. And soon.

By the time I get to the bottom of the mountain, most of what's carrying me is momentum from the incline. Finally, I make it to the end of the path and spot a locked ten-foot tall

Chapter One

chain-link fence dividing the mountain from the city streets.

Walking up and down the fence a bit, I search for a hole or a loose spot to get through, but there isn't one. Instead, I take a deep breath to summon all of the strength left in me. There's not much. I grip the twisted metal of the fence and heave myself up. It takes more energy than I thought it would—especially on an empty stomach—but I manage to get to the top and down the other side, half stumbling and adding yet another scrape to my side.

Now comes the next problem: where to go? I cross the street to a large concrete building, hearing the roar of traffic noise off in the distance. The towering buildings I spotted from the cave entrance rise up in the distance. Must be the center of town. The sun is setting, casting shadows in this deserted part of the city.

I come around the corner of the concrete building to a parking lot, where I spot a blonde woman walking briskly to her car with her keys clenched in her fist. She looks up from her phone and sees me, but only stops when I wave to her, unsure what else to do. I'm sure my grubby appearance isn't putting her at ease.

I consider telling her I need help—does my voice work? What does it sound like—but between two other vehicles, a man rushes out and grabs her from behind, pressing a gun against her side.

"Hey!" I bark as I take off in a run toward them. My throat feels like it's tearing with the shout, but I ignore it. The heat from my anger ripples through my body quickly as I race toward them. With only a few feet between us, I notice my hands are *literally* on fire.

But I don't burn. Or feel too hot. Instead, I feel a sense of confidence. A sense of purpose. A sense of *knowing* that I haven't had since I woke up in that cave.

The man stumbles backward as I charge him with my burning fists. He yanks his arm around the girl's neck and pulls her to the side, pointing his gun at me with his free hand, shaking. The girl screams when she sees me charge them.

In the moment, I don't worry about whether he'll shoot—he doesn't seem like the type of thug who has the balls to shoot anyway—and I follow through with a punch to his face.

He drops his gun, lets go of the girl, and recoils. "Son of a bitch!"

She backs away quickly, but still doesn't leave the scene.

The man growls and turns to me. My fists are no longer flames, although his face is blistering from the attack. He reaches for his gun, but a stream of fire shoots out of my palm to his hand, causing more of his skin to break out in blisters, just like his face.

He cries out in pain and eyes me up nervously, cradling his burnt appendage.

"Go!" My throat burns again from the force.

Without another word, he takes off running down the street.

My stomach growls and my muscles ache from the exhaustion I've felt since I woke up. Only now it's amplified with the extra exertion. Almost to a breaking point—quickly rising.

The girl takes a step forward. "Thank you. How did you—"

She doesn't finish her sentence as my energy is finally depleted and I collapse on the pavement in front of her.

Chapter Two

My skin prickles with goosebumps as I stir. It's freezing in here. Wherever *here* is. I'm getting tired of never knowing where I am. Scenes from my dreams continue to linger. I was back in the cave and someone else—*something* else—was in there with me, hidden in the shadows. It makes me glad that I'm awake.

I open my eyes and sit up, immediately feeling resistance. There are several plastic tubes stretched over my body. Some pieces are taped down across my chest. My tattered shirt has been removed, but I'm still filthy from head-to-toe.

A white curtain hangs from the ceiling and stretches around the bed I'm lying in, so I can't see much. The open steel support beams and ductwork above me tell me that I'm not in a hospital. There's a screen to my right that steadily chirps with each passing second.

I hear someone move on the other side of the curtain. Goosebumps prickle my skin again. What is this place? How did

I get here? Was I drugged? Am I hallucinating? *Why can't I remember who I am?*

The screen chirps faster as I begin to panic, pulling at the tubes stuck to my body, feeling the sting of pain shoot up my arm as I tear one away from the inside of my elbow, blood running down my skin.

"Woah! Woah!" The curtain swings open and the girl from the parking lot rushes in. She's in a white lab coat and baby blue plastic gloves. Not at all what I was expecting. "It's okay, just calm down. You're okay." She shushes me as her hand pushes at my chest and guides me back down on the bed. When she pulls her hand away, the palm of her glove is black from my dirty body.

"These are just a few monitors to make sure you're okay," she explains as she presses a piece of gauze against my bleeding arm. "If you don't want them, I'll take them off. I just wanted to make sure you were okay."

I nod slowly. The chirps begin to slow.

We're quiet as she tends to my self-inflicted injury. More goosebumps spread across my skin as she works. Her hands are warm, but it's only a further reminder how cold it is in here. My fingers and toes are nearly numb. With each touch, her gloves turn blacker from the soot covering me.

"Sorry about that," she says, as if reading my thoughts about the temperature. "Keeping a cooler temperature helps with some of our other experiments. And with what happened outside…"

So that *did* happen.

"I can find something to keep you warm if you like?"

I shake my head because I'm not sure what to say to her. I'm still debating whether I can trust her, but she seems sincere enough. Genuine. Good. Not to mention, she was the victim in that attack in the parking lot. Why would she hurt me if I saved her life?

"I'm Rachel." She pulls off the bloody, dirty gloves and tosses them in a bio trash receptacle. "What's your name?"

Chapter Two

Ash, I think, but I don't say it. Instead, her question hangs in the air.

She must get the message that I'm not going to respond to her, so she says, "Thanks for helping me out there. I wasn't paying attention. Thank God you came along."

Rachel turns her back to me and opens the curtain more, revealing a desk stacked with papers. Beyond it, there's a glass wall that looks out to another room with more desks and pieces of equipment.

What is this place?

Rachel leans over and writes something in a journal on the cluttered desk. Definitely not a defensive position, so she must not feel threatened by me. Maybe she *can* be trusted.

She turns back around and glances at my hands before meeting my eyes. She doesn't say anything else about the flames that burned at the end of my arms, but I know it's on her mind. It's on mine, too. How was that even possible? Rachel might not know the answer, but she seems like the type of person who would be curious to find out.

"So what happened to you?" She pulls out a fresh set of gloves. "You were extremely dehydrated, covered in soot, and your clothes are all torn. I threw your shirt out, by the way. There was practically nothing left of it. Do you want a hospital gown?"

A hospital gown? *Is* this a hospital?

I shake my head.

"Okay." She's quiet as she waits for my explanation. I don't give her one. "So what's going on? I'm guessing you weren't just out for a walk." She smirks and points to my feet. "Especially with only one shoe."

I smile, but that's all I'm willing to offer.

She waits for me to continue, but doesn't get any more from me. Her smile fades.

"Is there anyone I can call for you? Or you can call them yourself, too," she offers.

I shake my head again. There *could* be someone, but I can't remember them, let alone their phone number. For all I know, there's someone out there—maybe even in this city—who is worried about me. Someone who might be missing me. And I can't get to them because I can't remember who they are.

I feel stupid.

I feel helpless.

Behind Rachel, someone with dark curls and thick-rimmed black glasses steps into the room on the other side of the glass wall. He's wearing a green shirt with EIT printed across it. The logo looks familiar, but I can't place it. At least it's a sign that I still have something in my head.

The monitor to my right chirps faster again and I sit up higher in the bed. I don't like the way he's lingering. Do I know him? I don't know who I can trust.

Rachel looks over her shoulder and then back at me. "No, it's okay. That's Perry. He works here too."

My breathing eases up and I force myself to relax, but the chirps on the monitor still don't calm down. It doesn't help that I still haven't established where *here* is.

She turns back to him. "Thanks for coming."

He steps forward and asks, "Rachel, who is this?" He doesn't sound happy.

She looks between us. "Um…I don't know his name—"

He rolls his eyes and turns away as he looks at the ceiling.

"*But*," she continues, "he saved me from being mugged…or worse."

"Mugged?" Perry raises his eyebrows. "Where? What happened? Are you okay?"

"Yeah, I'm fine. It was in the parking lot—"

"Here?" he blurts.

"Yeah. This guy jumped me—"

"*This* guy?" He points to me.

"No, some other guy." She motions to me. "*He* saved me."

Chapter Two

Perry lets out a deep breath and drops his shoulders. He studies me for a long while and then turns back to her. "All right. I'm glad you're okay. But who is he and why is he in here?"

"He, uh, collapsed in front of me," she says.

"So why isn't he in a hospital?"

Guess that answers that question.

"There's more to it than that," she says.

"Like?" he pushes. "Is this why you called me? For protection?"

She looks down at the floor. Another question answered.

"Rach, if you didn't trust him, why would you bring him here?" he nearly shouts.

"Because he was hurt!" She glances over at me, suddenly realizing they're arguing about me right in front of me. "Look, I'll explain later," she tells him just before she turns back to me. "How are you feeling? Better?"

I nod. I feel awkward as her hands pull more monitor cords from my chest. I'm gross. I'm confused. I'm tired. I'm hungry.

So hungry.

"Well, you're not as dehydrated, but you still have a bit to go before I'd say you were back to full strength," she explains. "Can you talk?"

I glance up at Perry, who watches our interaction with a hard expression on his face and his arms crossed.

Rachel follows my look and then turns back to me. "Don't worry about him. If he's making you uncomfortable, I can ask him to leave."

"Like hell I will!" he shouts. "Rachel, you don't even know who this guy is!"

She shoots him a look. "Perry, please."

He puts up his hands and leans against the door frame.

She turns back to me. "Do you want me to ask him to leave?"

I shake my head.

"Can you talk?" she asks again.

I try to say, "Yeah," but it comes out all croaky. As if I was raised from the dead. Was I raised from the dead!?

No, the heart monitor indicated I'm very much alive.

She turns to her friend. "Can you get him a glass of water?"

He eyes me, but turns and disappears out of the room.

"Don't worry about him," she says when he's gone. "He's just suspicious because—well, it's kind of a suspicious situation. I mean, it's Sunday. It's late. I called him at home. Didn't tell him about you until he got here—my bad. I just couldn't leave you lying there and with..." She pauses, choosing her words carefully. "With what I saw, I didn't think a hospital was the best place for you." She chuckles. "You're just lucky that I decided to get some work done today instead of pushing it off until tomorrow."

I nod and try to say, "Thank you," but again, it's basically inaudible.

Perry returns with a glass of water and hands it to me. I consider the possibility that he put something in it, but if they were going to hurt me, they would've done it when I was unconscious. I really do think they're trying to help. At least, Rachel is.

The water is a refreshing relief on my throat and I guzzle down the whole glass. Rachel takes it from me and passes it to Perry.

"Can you get him some more? Please?"

He sighs loudly but takes the glass—careful not to touch the soot leftover from my hand—and disappears once more.

"Let's try this again." She smiles kindly. "Where did you come from before you saw me? You looked like you had been out in the desert. Were you lost or something?"

I shake my head. "Cave."

Better to try to communicate with as few words as possible. My voice obviously doesn't want to cooperate. The word feels tight in my throat, but at least it comes out clearly. The voice is a muscle and I haven't used mine in God only knows how long.

"A cave?" she asks. "Like in the mountains?"

Chapter Two

I nod.

"What were you doing up there?" she asks.

I shrug.

"Did you get lost?"

I shake my head. "Can't remember."

Her eyes narrow. "You can't remember what?"

Perry comes in and hands me the refilled glass. I drink some more, feeling my head clear with each passing gulp.

"Anything," I respond.

"Anything what?" Perry asks.

"Really?" She ignores him. "Nothing at all?"

"My name is Ash." I can already feel my voice getting tired just from these few words, but I owe her some sort of explanation. She might be able to help me find some answers.

Rachel turns to Perry. "He doesn't remember anything."

He rolls his eyes. "Convenient."

She shoots him another look—she's good at that. "Just...give him a chance, okay?"

He sighs and nods. "Amnesia?"

"That's what I'm thinking," she says.

"How can we be sure?"

"We can't, but he saved my life."

Noticeably, he backs down. "Okay. You're right. We'll have to consider all of our options." He looks at me. "In the meantime, you're filthy and should probably get cleaned up before you start contaminating stuff."

"Thank you," I say.

He gives me a half smile—the most I've gotten from him yet.

"Would you mind taking him down to the locker room and keeping an eye on him?" Rachel asks Perry. "I don't want him to slip or anything."

"Since when is watching a stranger shower in my job description?" he asks.

She rolls her eyes. "Just be in the same room. There should

be some extra soap and stuff in the utility closet in the basement. You have some extra clothes he can borrow, right?"

He sighs again. "I guess so."

"Good, thanks." She turns to me and puts her gloved hand on my soot-covered arm. "Perry's going to take you to get cleaned up. That should help you feel a little better."

She stands in front of me and holds out her hands for mine to help me up. I take them, but it's unnecessary. I can walk on my own, although my stomach still growls. My head is pretty clear, too, considering everything I've been through in the last several hours.

"Are you hungry? I'll call for takeout," she says. "Go on with Perry and it'll be waiting when you get back."

Perry grabs ahold of my elbow until we're out of view of Rachel and then lets go, wiping his hand in his jeans. "You good on your own?"

I nod. "Yeah, I'm fine."

"Good."

"What is this place?" The words come a little easier now.

"This is the Ellsworth Science and Technology Research lab, or ESTR for short," he says. "Basically, we develop ways to make human life easier, be that with scientific breakthroughs or technological advancements."

"Ellsworth is the city?" That piece of knowledge seems to be hidden behind a thin veil that separates certainty with uncertainty.

"Uh-huh," he says with a nod. "Are you from here?"

I shrug. "I don't know. I think so?"

We reach the staircase at the end of the hall and he holds the door for me.

"You're really not kidding about this amnesia thing, are you?" He flicks on some lights.

I shake my head as we descend the stairs. "No, I really have no idea who I am. I don't like it."

Chapter Two

"I can't blame you."

At the bottom of the stairs, he holds open another door that leads to a large open basement. More lights kick on. The boiler sits in one corner, the electrical equipment in another, and the rest of the space is filled with storage. Desks, chairs, metal work tables, filing cabinets presumably filled with folders, and tons of research equipment. On either side of the staircase door sits locker rooms for men and women.

Perry bypasses them, though, and goes to a metal storage cabinet on the far wall, meandering around forgotten desks and tables. He looks through the assortment of cleaners and other chemicals and snatches up a box filled with small bottles and passes them to me.

"Here, double check that these are shampoo bottles. You can never be too careful about what people stash in here."

I pull out a bottle and sniff. It smells nice. Hesitantly, I dab my finger in the goo.

"Yeah, it's good."

"Good." He walks over to a set of lockers and cradles the lock as he dials in the code. He opens the door and pulls out a towel and some clothes. "These are the only set of clothes I have here, so I want these back, *capish*?"

I take them from him and nod. "I will, thanks. I really do appreciate this." I don't want to think about where I'd be if Rachel hadn't taken me in.

He points to the men's locker room. "I think you can figure out the shower on your own. I'll wait out here."

Inside, I peel off my crusty clothes and toss them in the trash. I want to put as much distance between me and the memories of the cave as I can. Not to mention, those clothes were ruined.

The soap points out each scrape on my body, burning until it's thoroughly washed away. I have a lot more abrasions than I thought. Mostly on my torso and hands, but there's a decent scrape on my leg, too.

Besides the stinging wounds, the shower feels amazing. It feels so good to be free of the soot and grime that's been coating my body since I woke up. How long has it been since I've had a proper shower? It's anyone's guess. I'm going to take advantage.

With a towel wrapped around me, I finally take a good look at myself in the mirror. My blond hair is darkened by the water still soaked in it. I'm thinner than I thought, but not scrawny. Maybe I'm an athlete? Or maybe just young? I have to *at least* be in my twenties. I don't *feel* like a teenager and my ability to wake up in a rocky cave without too many aches tells me I'm not older than my twenties. But would anyone actually feel their age if they didn't know?

What's most noticeable, though, are the number of scrapes and bruises all over my body. Nothing too bad, but certainly more than I expected—even with the burning reminders in the shower. My right shoulder especially has a significant bruise from when I woke up in the cave.

I shake my head, ridding myself of the memory. I'm never going back to that cave. Not willingly, anyway.

Still, the thought of what *could've* happened in that cave makes me realize just how lucky I am to be standing here, somewhere seemingly safe, with seemingly good people. God only knows how I ended up where I did. Chances are, I didn't just wander in there on my own. I'm grateful that I was able to get out and don't have any lingering injuries—at least, none that I know of.

Perry's clothes fit me well. Just an old band T-shirt—someone I've never heard of—and a pair of gym shorts. I have to tie the drawstring tight, but otherwise they fit.

"All set?" Perry's leaning against the wall opposite the men's locker room, scrolling through a small handheld device.

"Yeah. What is that?"

"What is what?"

I point.

Chapter Two

"My phone?" He scrunches his eyebrows.

"Oh." I feel kind of stupid for not knowing, but it doesn't look anything like a phone. More like a flat box.

"You really have lost your mind, haven't you?"

"Guess so." I could go without the constant reminders, though.

We make our way back up to Lab Room #8, bypassing Labs 1-7 along the way. It's a small room with another room off of it, one being the medic room I woke up in. There's a very large TV mounted on the far wall and Rachel and another man study it. Someone I haven't seen before. He's older than the three of us, with short graying hair. He has white khaki shorts and a blue T-shirt tucked in.

"What are you guys watching?" Perry asks.

"Come here." Rachel plays with the necklace under her chin.

"Is that outside?" he asks.

"This is live," the man says.

I step forward and watch. It's nothing like anything I've ever seen before. Through the billows of black smoke and thick storm cloud, I can see fire raining down from the sky, igniting the city below.

Chapter Three

Something bursts inside me, almost like an instinct. I step closer to the screen and ask, "Where is this happening?"

The fear in Rachel's voice makes it nearly a whisper. "Everywhere."

Perry goes to another monitor and within a few seconds, an aerial view of the city appears with red areas scattered across the map.

"She's not kidding," he says. "It's starting fires all over the city."

"The fire department can't respond to all of those fast enough," the man says.

"What are we going to do?" Rachel asks, her voice rising in panic. "What if it hits us? Or our houses?"

"I don't know, but we have to do something." Perry points to a section on the map. "Look, there's fire falling right outside. This thing could hit the old coal mines, meaning that the whole mountain could blow up."

Chapter Three

"But what is it?" Rachel moves to another monitor and taps away at the keyboard.

"Isn't there something you guys can come up with to stop it?" the man asks.

"There's not enough time!" she panics.

I can't just sit here and watch as fire rains down on the city. The news shows homes ablaze, people running scared, trees burning. A city that was settling in for the night moments ago is now in chaos.

Before I have another thought, I race down the hallway in search of the door. I don't know if I can stop the fires, but I can at least help get people to safety.

"Hey!" Perry calls to me from down the hall. He jogs the length of the hallway to reach me. He grabs my arm and I stop. "Where are you going?"

Rachel and the other man are right behind him.

"I'm going out to help," I say.

"You're going to get yourself killed," the man says.

"Vernon," Rachel says to him as a warning. She takes a step closer to me. "If you go out there with your...ability, people might think that *you* started the fires."

"Ability?" the man—Vernon—asks, but we both ignore him.

"But there are people getting hurt," I say. "And since I do have this ability, maybe it'll help prevent any criminals from taking advantage of this mess."

The guys both look confused.

"What do you think you're going to do that the rest of us can't?" Perry asks. "Our efforts are better spent in here, hunkering down until this storm passes."

I have a sinking suspicion that this is not a storm but something that was caused from my escape from the cave. I don't share that theory, though. Instead, I turn to Rachel, trying to communicate the urgency of this with my eyes.

"Let him go," she finally says.

"What?" Vernon asks.

"We're just wasting time," she reasons. "If he wants to go help out there, then let him. We'll do what we can from in here."

There's a crash above us. Must be the fire rain has hit the building.

"I'll go close the air vents." Vernon rushes down the hall.

Perry runs back to Lab #8. "I'm going to try to figure out what kind of storm this is."

I start toward the door again, but Rachel reaches for my arm. "Be careful. Come back here if you need help, okay?"

I nod. "I will. Thank you."

Could this be the last time I see the woman who saved me from starvation?

She points down the hall. "The door on the right just before the elevator will take you out to the employee parking lot. It *won't* let you back in. You'll have to go around to the main entrance on the other side of the building. I'll keep my eye on the cameras for you."

I give her another nod. "Okay."

The heat is the first thing I notice even before I step through the door, but it's impossible to miss the ominous sky. Although gray with the setting sun, several large glowing white orbs float in the air, shooting out streaks of fire that fall down to the city and cast unnatural colors throughout the atmosphere.

I follow one stream of fire as it falls from the orb toward a car parked across the street from ESTR. There's a woman inside, crying from fear.

Racing to her, I fling the car door open and grab her arm, pulling her on top of me on the pavement, just as the fire stream collides with her car. Thankfully, she wasn't buckled. We scramble back as the fire consumes her vehicle, sending thick black smoke into the air.

Her breath is ragged as she watches her car burn.

I help her to her feet. "Go! Find someplace to get shelter!"

Chapter Three

She nods and takes off, too scared to offer a thanks.

There's a loud bang behind me and when I spin around, I see another white orb has opened up a few feet above the street. Someone in a black trench coat and a leather mask steps out and the orb disappears behind him.

"Ah, so you *are* here, Ash."

Pain suddenly fills my head, concentrated between my eyes. It's like a bad brain freeze, but worse. I double over, clutching my head, and suddenly the flaming city around me seems to fade for a moment as my mind fills with images of myself when I was a kid—it's too familiar not to be my memory.

There's another boy, about the same age as me, pinned under my knees as I punch his chest over and over again. He's screaming, telling me to stop. His arms squirm under me, but he doesn't have the strength to push me off. Over and over again, I punch him until he starts crying.

I'm not sure how much more of this pain in my head I can take as it seems to get worse the longer the image plays out. Finally, gentle hands grasp my arms, pulling me off the boy, and just as quickly, I'm pulled out of myself.

The throbbing between my eyes passes and I stare at the cracked street I've fallen to, trying to catch my breath. I don't have time to regain my composure, though. Suddenly, the street is gone and everything goes black. I'm falling, with nothing to stop myself until the world comes back in an instant and I crash on my side, closer to the apocalyptic sky than I was before.

The change in scenery leaves me disoriented and I lay on the rough surface, staring as balls of flame erupt from the orbs above me. Under the glow of the fire, the world is bright up here.

With creaky limbs, I get to my feet and look around. I'm on top of the ESTR building, I think. The mountain I escaped from is close. One corner of the roof is burning from one of the fire blasts. I start to run toward it, but another orb opens beneath me and I step into it and suddenly I'm free falling again. When

I come through the other side, I land flat on my back against the pavement of the street by the burning car I just rescued the woman from. I land with the same force as if I had just tripped on the sidewalk. Wherever I go in these orbs, gravity's not much of a factor.

Ignoring my disorientation, I jump up again and try to run toward the main door of ESTR. I'm only a few feet away and then—I step into another orb, somersaulting across the roof of a high rise downtown, finally coming to a stop right on the edge.

My body shakes with nerves as it hits me that I'm literally inches from death—my right leg dangles off the side. I can even feel the heat from the storm licking my face. It only adds to the nervous sweat I break out into.

Rolling away from the edge, I start to crawl to the center of the building so I can get to my feet, but once again, I slip into another portal. Over and over again, I fall into the orbs, throwing me in different directions that I'm unable to anticipate. My head spins with confusion.

Finally, I fall through another one and land on the cracked street in front of ESTR. Again. I stare at the ground on my hands and knees and try to make my vision stop spinning. It's not working. I'm sick on the cement and crawl away slowly. My eyes land on the boots of the man in the trench coat, trailing up his body until our eyes meet. He steps closer.

"What's the matter?" he asks. "Did you not enjoy the ride?"

"Why are you bombing the city like this?" I ask in a ragged voice. My body's still weak from the cave, not to mention the joyride I just took around town.

"I needed to draw you out somehow," he says. "See if my suspicions were true."

"Suspicions?" I rise to my knees. "What are you—I don't even know you! Why are you doing this?"

"You know *exactly* why!" He extends his arm, but for once I'm anticipating his move.

Chapter Three

From head to toe, my body bursts into flames and I shoot up into the air away from him. I hover above the city for a moment, looking down at all the burning buildings.

Houses, vehicles, trees, the fires are relentless. The streets are crowded with people, all looking for safety. Fire truck sirens blare. The sound of crackling fire across the city carries up to me. All because this man in the trench coat wanted to draw me out.

Angry, I sweep back around with the intention of firing an attack at the man, but the lack of food and sleep catches up with me and I feel myself weaken. The flames sputter out for moments at a time until I land hard in a dumpster in the parking lot of ESTR, luckily no longer on fire.

My body's stiff as I begin to stir. I'm sore, but nothing feels broken. Peering over the edge of the dumpster, I look for traces of the man in the trench coat, but my vision is pulled upward.

One by one, the orbs dissipate and the sky grows dark once again.

Chapter Four

"Your pulse is normal." Rachel removes the pressure cuff from my arm and pulls down my eyelid. "Pupil's aren't dilated."

"Guys, I'm fine." I'm sitting on the exam table in the medic room. I have a towel wrapped around my waist and a lab coat over my shoulders. Turns out when I completely burst into flame, my body can sustain it but my clothes cannot. Luckily, Vernon agreed to run home to get me something to wear.

Perry sits at a monitor in the next room and watches the footage from the outside camera that shows my body erupting in flame. Again and again he replays it, studying it without a word. He can't hide the big grin on his face, though.

Rachel looks at me, fresh out of explanations. I notice that she keeps her distance. "Ash, what happened was—"

"Impossible," Perry finishes. "There's no way you should be able to do that." He gets up and joins us in the medic room.

"Well, I did," I say. "And I don't really know how, either. I was

Chapter Four

just...angry. A little scared, but mostly angry."

Rachel glances at Perry, worry very evident on her face.

"Angry at what?" she asks. "At that man? Do you know him?"

"No, but I hated the fact that he was kicking my ass."

"Dude, earlier today you were trapped in a cave." Perry stands beside Rachel with his arms crossed. At least he doesn't seem too worried about me. Not anymore at least. "Give yourself a break. Of course he was kicking your ass."

"I actually think you held your own," she adds quietly.

He smiles and looks me over. "You were *on fire*. Literally. Don't you realize how *awesome* this is?"

Rachel heads back into the other room.

"I guess." My stomach growls. "Maybe I'm just hungry."

"I'll text Vernon and tell him to pick up a pizza on the way." She cradles her phone in her hands—another flat box like Perry's—and watches us through the windows between the two rooms. "Hopefully something will still be open."

I get up and follow her into the next room, careful to keep a hand on the towel. "What's the matter?"

She raises her eyebrows. "Me?"

"Yeah, you seem—I don't know, nervous."

She taps her phone screen with her thumb and then slides it in her lab coat. "It's just...what you did out there was...unusual."

Perry brushes by me on his way back to his computer. "Very much so."

"And from here it seemed like you knew what you were doing," she continues.

"Not really," I plead. "He got away!"

"I know, but it's just...are you *sure* you didn't know you could do that?" she pushes.

"Positive. I swear, I was just as surprised as you were."

That seems to satisfy her.

"Okay." She offers a disarming smile. "I just needed to be sure."

I nod and our conversation hangs in the air for a few seconds until Perry breaks the silence from his desk.

"The fires are all out. The news said there was minimal damage."

"Really?" Rachel asks. "That's odd, but I'm glad. Any injuries?"

He nods. "A few, but nothing too bad."

Her phone buzzes again.

"What's that?" I ask.

"A text from Vernon."

"Text?"

She turns it to me and I see bubbles in different colors displayed. "Yeah, a text."

"Oh." I try to play it off like I know what she's talking about, but I have no idea. How come I remember some things but not others?

"He said he'll be back as soon as he can," she tells us.

"Is he a scientist too?" I ask.

Perry laughs. "He certainly thinks he is."

"No, he's not," Rachel explains. "The lab is funded by the investment company Vernon works for: River Valley Holdings. He's just our account manager there and he has a personal interest in what we do here."

I nod. "So he doesn't work here at all?"

"No, but that doesn't stop him from popping in all the time," Perry mutters.

Rachel smirks. "Like I said: personal interest."

"Gotcha."

"Yeah," she says. "If it's okay, I want to take a look at your blood. Maybe the answer to why you're…combustible is in your DNA."

"You want to take my blood?" I ask nervously.

"Don't tell me you're scared of that!" Perry says. "You just faced off against a guy who dropped fire from the sky!"

Chapter Four

"Are you sure they're all out?" From what I saw from my various vantage points, the fires seemed pretty widespread.

Rachel rolls to another monitor and turns on the news. I watch as cameras pan across a neighborhood of scorched houses, but none ablaze.

"How is that possible?" I ask.

Perry scrunches his eyebrows. "You didn't put them out?"

I shake my head. "No. I didn't have time. That guy showed up right away."

"That guy in the trench coat?" she asks.

"Yeah."

"Interesting," he notes, still furrowing his brow. "So this weird stuff didn't start until just before this…trench coat guy who could open portals—let's call him, um…the Gatekeeper. Yeah, that sounds good."

Rachel rolls her eyes.

"Anyway, so this weird stuff started just before the Gatekeeper actually showed up—"

"Actually, this portal guy—" Rachel starts, but Perry cuts her off.

"The Gatekeeper."

"Whatever. He didn't show up until *after* Ash went out to help people."

"He did say he was trying to draw me out, but he didn't say why." I still don't know *how* I fit in to this place, but clearly I *do* fit in here somehow.

Rachel raises her eyebrows and exchanges glances with Perry.

"I just thought—I don't think—this doesn't make sense!" I stutter.

"Ash, you must know him from *somewhere*," Rachel pushes. "Didn't he look at all familiar?"

I don't want to tell her about that memory I had when I first saw him. At least not while she's still not sure if she can trust me. I don't know if it was actually my past and what it means if it is.

Especially since I was the one beating the crap out of that kid.

Instead, I say, "Pardon me, but I'm pretty sure I would know if that was my first time *throwing fire* at someone."

"*The Gatekeeper!*" Perry urges.

"Whatever!" I shout at him. Maybe it's my lack of sleep or my hunger, but my fuse is quite short right now. Then again, it could also be the fact that I wasn't able to stop that man and I don't know who I am. "Besides, he was wearing a mask," I add.

Rachel takes a deep breath just before rising to her feet. "We'll just have to keep thinking then. Try to find out who is under that mask." Apparently, she senses my annoyance. She crosses the room to a work table along the wall and opens a drawer. "In the meantime, I need a sample of your blood."

I gulp and slowly walk over to her as she slips on two pairs of latex gloves and readies several vials.

She has me sit on a stool and I pull up the sleeve of the lab coat, diverting my eyes. She wipes a spot on my arm with alcohol.

"Don't be a baby." She slides the needle in and I wince. "I know you're tougher than that."

After several vials are filled, she presses a piece of gauze to the spot and instructs me to hold it down while she packs up the samples.

From the stool, I watch the rest of the news program as Perry and Rachel examine my blood at one of the work tables. The news reporters interview someone whose house caught on fire from the Gatekeeper's attacks—I guess that's as good a name as any. The resident says that only the one side of his house caught on fire. It ruined the siding, but he said he's just happy everyone's okay.

Another resident says a window was smashed after a fireball struck the street in front of her house, sending sparks shooting from the ground. Other than melted linoleum and shattered glass, no one was hurt.

I guess it helps me feel a little less guilty about being the cause of the attack. It's just infuriating that I don't even know *why* the Gatekeeper wanted to draw me out.

"I'm back!" Vernon's voice carries from the main entrance.

The smell of hot pizza grows stronger the closer he gets to us. I hop up from the chair, clutch at the loosening towel around my waist, and rush to him.

"I'm *starving*!" I grab the box from him.

"Careful, it's hot," he warns.

I don't care. I take a slice and chomp down a huge bite, feeling the hot cheese and sauce burn the inside of my mouth. Doesn't matter. Totally worth it.

"That took you a while," Perry says over his shoulder. He's still hunched over a microscope.

"Daniela was happy to see me after the fire storm," he says. "I guess she was worried that I was trapped somewhere."

"How is it out there?" Rachel asks.

He scrunches his face. "There's certainly been widespread fires, but the fire department seems to have it all under control."

"That's good," Perry says.

Vernon sets a canvas bag of clothes in front of me. "Oh, these are for you. I had to find a good combination of my clothes and my son's clothes to make sure they'd fit." He pats his round belly. "I think about two of you could fit in my pants."

Rachel comes over and grabs herself a piece of pizza. "I'm sure anything would be better than what he's wearing now."

"Which is nothing," Perry adds. "So much for getting my clothes back."

"Sorry," I say around a mouthful of pizza.

"I just wanted him to be comfortable," Vernon says to Rachel.

"Well thanks," I say, just before sinking my teeth into the doughy crust. Man, I missed food. Possibly a little too much. Maybe I was in that cave longer than I realized.

Vernon motions to the bag he brought with him. "You'll probably want to put these on."

I scarf down the rest of the slice and point to the box on one of the work tables. "I'm definitely having more. Don't eat it all."

Rachel smiles. "Don't worry." She points around the corner. "There's a bathroom down the hall to the left."

Snatching up the bag, I head off to change. In the bathroom, I search through my options. These clothes don't even look like something Vernon has worn in a long time. Threadbare sweatpants and an oversized T-shirt. But I guess I can't complain. I *did* burn off the last set I was given and these are still better than wearing just a towel.

I pull on the sweats, tie it at the waist to keep them from sliding off me. After I pull the T-shirt over my head and tuck it into the sweats, I look in the mirror. The shirt is huge, the collar hanging further down my chest than normal and the sleeves reach my elbows. But I guess beggars can't be choosers.

On the way back down the hall, the sound of my name stops me in my tracks.

"...Ash could be a danger to us," Vernon says.

"He's had ample time to do something if that was his intention," Perry says.

"And he seems genuinely appreciative of everything we're doing for him," Rachel adds. "And I believe him that he had nothing to do with the attacks."

"That's just it," Vernon counters. "It's only been a few hours and look what's already happened."

It's quiet. Until now, I hadn't considered it much that they might see me as a threat. *I* know I'm not, but have I convinced *them* of that yet? Obviously not Vernon.

"Look, he might be able to create fire or worse, we're not sure exactly, but so far he's only ever used those abilities to help people," Perry says.

"Well," Rachel's voice is small, "he *did* say that the Gatekeeper said he was looking for Ash, which is why he set fire to the whole city."

Chapter Four

"How do we know that wasn't Ash?" Vernon asks. "We already know he can throw fire. How do we know he's not tricking us for whatever reason? What if he's playing dumb?"

"He's not," Perry says.

"We have to consider it," Rachel counters, which stings. I thought she was on my side. But then, like Vernon's pointed out, I've only known them a few hours.

"Okay, so let's say Ash *isn't* trying to do anything bad to us," Vernon says. "If this Gatekeeper guy has targeted him once, what's saying he won't do it again? And how are we supposed to be equipped to help? What happens if we wake up tomorrow and ESTR is gone, along with Ash? How would you feel then?"

"I didn't think he'd stay here tonight," Rachel says quietly.

"And you're just going to bring a strange man into your house?" Vernon asks.

She raises her voice a bit. "It beats leaving him scared and alone here."

"So that you can die in the privacy of your own home?"

"That's not going to happen."

"Guys, I think he'll be fine," Perry says over both of them

I step out from the hall. "I think Vernon has a point."

Rachel's shoulders drop when she sees me. Perry turns away and Vernon sits up straighter.

"How much of that did you hear?" Rachel asks quietly.

"Enough to decide that Vernon's right," I reply. "You guys haven't known me that long. There's no reason for you to trust me."

"Ash, that's not what we think," Rachel says.

"Come on, it's getting late," Perry says. "I'll set you up on the couch at my place and we'll talk about it again in the morning. And get you into some better clothes. What's with the T-shirt tucked in?" He turns and looks at Vernon. "Is that really the best you could find?"

I shake my head. "No, I think I should stay somewhere else

tonight." Mentally, I make a note not to tuck my shirt in anymore.

"Ash," Vernon says. "I didn't mean to…I meant, you're just… you weren't here this morning and now—"

"He needs a place to stay, Vernon," Rachel tells him. "At least for tonight until we can get some more answers."

"I'll set him up at a hotel," Vernon says.

She shakes her head. "No. You said it yourself, the Gatekeeper would find him overnight. The chances of that happening when he's with someone else are slimmer."

"Why doesn't he just stay with you?" Perry asks Vernon. "You seem to be the most worried about him. This way you can keep an eye on him yourself. You have more people living with you that they can keep an eye on him too."

"My family?" Vernon's voice grows.

"Guys, I don't want to cause an argument," I say. "But Rachel's right, I *do* need a place to sleep. I don't remember really anything about this city—or anyone in it—so you tell me: where am I going to go? I wouldn't mind a hotel."

"You're not going to a hotel," Rachel says definitively, but offers no other alternative.

It's quiet again as they all stare at the floor. Finally, Vernon speaks up.

"Okay. He can stay with me for tonight. We'll see how it goes." He checks his watch. "Perry's right. It *is* getting late and we should probably get going."

I yawn, as if on cue.

"Go and get some rest," Rachel says. "We'll see what we can find in the morning."

Chapter Five

The drive to Vernon's house is my first real exploration of the city. Once we cross the river, we meander past a large cylinder building and a few other towers—one of them I nearly fell off of thanks to the Gatekeeper. Within two turns, the streets are lined with trees creating a barrier between the cars and the large mansions along the street.

Vernon pulls into the driveway of one and drives along the side of the red brick building to the carriage house-style garage in the back. He cuts the engine and opens the door. "I texted my wife that you were coming over so she shouldn't be surprised to see you."

"Texted, right." I step out and follow him out the garage door.

As we step closer to the house, I'm quiet. He's already made it known that he's nervous about me, so I don't want to do or say anything that might add to that.

We enter the house through a back door that opens into a pristine white kitchen. The only hints of color are the large paintings hanging above the breakfast nook to the right and the mosaic tile inset into the subway tile backsplash behind the stove. Contrary to the cold appearance, the room is quite warm.

Fading scents from dinner linger. The dishwasher hums. The lights have been dimmed.

"Rosa must've already cleaned up," Vernon says. "She's our cook."

I nod politely. I might not remember exactly who I was before, but I do know that I didn't come from a place where someone else cooks for you.

"This way." He leads me though a swinging door into a large dining room.

The polished hardwood floorboards creak beneath our feet as we walk. There's a large antique dining table in the center of the room. Situated in the middle is a decorative plant with candlesticks on either side.

There's a sitting room at the front of the house, tucked in the corner. I follow Vernon in, where a beautiful dark-skinned woman lounges on an ornate couch with a book in her hand. When she spots me, she immediately sits up, her finger in the book to mark her place.

"Oh, hello," she stammers. Folding down the corner of one of the pages, she sets the book on the table and steps forward to shake my hand. "I'm Daniela."

"Ash," I say with a smile.

Vernon steps forward and kisses his wife.

"Are you home for the night then?" she asks him.

"Should be, yeah," he says. "Sorry about earlier. There was a, uh, accident at the lab and it ruined some of Ash's clothes so I needed to come home and get him a new set."

"Accident?"

"The fires," I add.

She nods. "My apologies, Ash. My husband hasn't mentioned you before. I take it you've just started working at the research lab?"

Chapter Five

"Uh..." I look to Vernon for help. He looks at me, waiting for my answer. "Yeah," I finally say. "It hasn't been long."

"What do you study?"

This time, he does come to my rescue. "Ash has had a long day. I think it's probably best if he gets settled in."

"Settled in?" she asks.

"Yeah. He needs a place to stay for a bit."

Daniela gives her husband a stern look and then offers me a smile. "Would you mind giving us a minute?"

"Where are the kids?" Vernon asks.

"Uh, in the living room, I suppose," she replies.

Vernon points across the dining room and says, "They should be through that doorway. You should go introduce yourself."

I would like to do anything else, but I can tell they need some time alone.

The TV is on in the living room, but both teenagers, a boy and a girl, are staring at their phones. The room is dark and only the glow from the large TV illuminates the room.

I clear my throat to get their attention. "Uh, your dad wanted me to come and introduce myself."

As soon as the words leave my mouth, I wish I would've just stayed in the dining room and waited for Vernon to get done talking to his wife.

"Who are you?" the boy asks.

"I'm Ash. I, uh, work with your father—well, sort of. Not really, I guess."

"At the lab?" the girl asks.

I nod. "Yeah. With Rachel and Perry."

They nod.

"Yeah." I glance back out toward the front sitting room, but there's no sign of Vernon.

Reluctantly, I take a seat in the closest chair and stare at the TV. Some kind of endurance challenge, it looks like. The image is crisp, the screen is large, and they look like they're about to jump out at us at any moment. Several times, I flinch as the camera moves closer to the athletes.

"So did you see the fire storm then?" the boy asks.

"Yeah, I saw it."

"Pretty cool, huh?"

"If by 'pretty cool' you mean terrifying, sure."

They both give me side-eyes before turning back to the TV. Other than the screen, the room goes painfully quiet. Yep, definitely should've just stayed in the dining room.

"Ah, I see you three have gotten acquainted," Vernon's voice breaks into the awkward silence.

I jump to my feet.

"Hope you kids have treated Ash well," he says, but neither of them look up at him. "He'll be staying with us for a bit."

That grabs their attention.

"Seriously?" the girl grumbles.

"Amelia, don't be rude," Vernon scolds. "He needs a place to stay and we have more than enough room."

"He's not going to have to sleep in my room, is he?" the boy asks.

"No, I'm going to put him in the guest room at the top of the stairs." He turns to me. "Speaking of which, you're probably tired, so I'll show you up to your room. Peter, Amelia, say goodnight."

"'Night," they both mutter right before I eagerly follow Vernon out of the room.

Who knew such a nice house would make me feel so uncomfortable? I can't wait to get to my own room and unwind with no one but myself.

The door right at the top of the winding stairs leads into a small guest bedroom. A four-poster bed sits in the middle with an antique dresser that matches the dining room table nestled in the corner. The white carpet makes me glad that I already had a shower.

"It's not much, but it's what we've got," Vernon says. He points to another door. "That's your own bathroom. I can have one of the girls bring up a fresh set of towels."

I offer a tight smile. At least he's trying, but I still feel weird taking advantage of his hospitality when he made it clear that he's afraid of the trouble I might bring.

"I'm sure the kids will warm up to you eventually," he says. "And I explained what I could to Daniela—I left out the part about you being, well, you know. There's no way she'd let you stay if she..." He trails off. "Anyway..."

"Thanks for letting me stay here tonight," I say.

"No problem. I hope you'll find it comfortable."

"I'm sure I will."

"There are more blankets in the closet across the hall, in case you need them," he offers. "But with this heat, I'm not sure you will."

I nod, not sure what else to say. I just want to crawl into that large bed and fall asleep.

Tomorrow I can explore. All I've seen since I woke up in the cave was the inside of ESTR and now Vernon's house. Well, that's if you don't count the psycho attack from the Gatekeeper. Hopefully, he doesn't know where I am.

As if sensing my desire to explore, he asks, "How about tomorrow I show you around town? We could stop and get you some clothes that you actually like. I could show you some of the Ellsworth hotspots."

"Maybe, yeah."

Again, he's trying. I need to give him that much. Especially if he's letting me stay here when he doesn't completely trust me. Can't say I blame him. If spending a day with him sets his mind at ease, then that's what I'll have to do. It's not like I have anything else planned.

"Well, I'll leave you be to get some rest." He steps to the

door and swings it open. "Good night."

When he's gone, I kick off my shoes, lie back on the bed, and fall asleep within minutes.

"THE VIEW IS beautiful up here." Vernon sets his leg on a rock and leans on his knee, breathing heavy.

We're on the Rim Trail along the mountain on the east side of the city. From here, I can see the streets and buildings laid out between this mountain and the dreaded western mountain, where the cave was that I woke up in. Vernon thought I should spend my first official day in Ellsworth exploring the city. I think he just wanted an excuse to take a day off, but then, he could also be trying to make up for last night's initial distrust.

"Wow, this is incredible," I say, noting that I'm not nearly as breathless as Vernon is. "No wonder people decided to build a city here."

He nods and wipes the sweat from his brow. "You see the Ellsworth National Bank building there? That cylinder one?"

I follow where he's pointing to and spot the tower he's talking about. "That's the one we were just in, right? The one with the observation deck?"

He nods again, limiting his words, apparently. "If we follow this trail, we'll actually be taller than that tower."

"That's cool."

"Yeah." He eyes up the path to the peak and then back down the way we came. "Do you want to hike up anymore or are you good?"

I decide not to embarrass him by pointing out his athletic inabilities, so I agree to head back down.

We don't talk about much—we haven't really all day. I slept in until about ten, had breakfast with Rosa, the cook, and Daniela. Well, Daniela had coffee and read a magazine, only offering short pleasantries when it was impossible to ignore my presence. I get it. My stay was sprung on her.

Luckily, though, Vernon left work early and rescued me from the house. I was hoping to go to ESTR to see if Rachel and Perry came up with any answers about who I am, how I can throw fire, or why I don't remember anything, but I figured a day away from the insanity wouldn't hurt.

Once we get back down to the car, Vernon blasts the air conditioning. I don't remember that the technology even existed. I really need answers.

"So, where to now?" I ask.

Vernon guzzles down the rest of his water. "I should've brought this up there with me." When it's gone, he tosses it in his back seat and says, "Uh, I could show you Center Park downtown, if you want. I mean, we drove by it earlier, but it is quite something when you get out and walk around."

I remember from before. It was a weird feeling to be surrounded by so many tall buildings. I'm not sure if I've ever experienced anything like that. Maybe I have, but don't remember.

"No, it's okay." I shake my head. "I'm actually still quite tired, so I probably should get back so I can take a shower and a nap."

He nods, a hint of relief on his face. "Okay, sure, no problem." He shifts into gear and pulls onto the road, back to that uncomfortable house that's the closest thing I have to a home.

Chapter Six

"Still regret not coming with Vernon?" Rachel asks a few hours later in the mall food court. She licks up a spoonful of mint chocolate chip ice cream.

The place is crowded with evening shoppers, all taking a break to enjoy a quick dinner. We've hit up several stores and found me an assortment of clothes, some of which I'm wearing already because Rachel said I just *had* to stop wearing sweat-pants in public. I was inclined to agree. Instead, she picked out a pair of jeans and a red V-neck T-shirt.

"Well, I do think I missed an opportunity to mimic his ward-robe," I joke. I dive into my own dish. Vanilla, to keep things simple.

After my nap—and after he had time to recoup from our day's adventures—Vernon offered to take me to the mall to buy new clothes. Luckily, Rachel showed up after she got out of work and offered to do the same. Since I spent the day with Vernon, I didn't feel guilty about turning him down.

Chapter Six

She laughs.

"No, seriously. Thanks for saving me from that house."

"That bad, huh?"

"For a place that looks so beautiful, you'd think it'd be more inviting."

She shakes her head. "Meh, not really. No, Vernon's family is nice…in their own way. They're not really *people* people…does that make sense?"

I laugh. "If I hadn't met them it wouldn't have."

"You'll survive another night," she says. "And even another morning. We'll make other arrangements for tomorrow."

"Thanks," I say. "I mean, really. About everything. The last twenty-four hours have been so…weird."

She raises her eyebrows and nods. "You're not kidding. I was on my way home last night for a quiet night in until you showed up."

"Actually, it was that guy who tried to rob you," I clarify.

"But you saved me," she says with a bright smile. "Twice, actually."

"The Gatekeeper wouldn't have hurt you, specifically." I look down at the remnants of my ice cream—another delicacy I forgot I missed. "He only showed up because of me."

Rachel shakes her head. "Enough. That's tomorrow's problem. Tonight our mission was to find you clothes, which we've accomplished."

I motion to the bags sitting beside my chair. "And we certainly did. Thanks for buying me all this stuff."

She waves it off. "If you don't wear it, I know someone who could."

"You think Perry would wear some of this?"

"There have only been a handful of times that I've seen him in anything other than an old T-shirt and jeans," she says. "But, it *would* make up for you *burning* his clothes."

"True. Do you think he's still mad about that?"

"If he's not, he will be soon. He doesn't really hold grudges like that. Anyway, are you excited about your loot?"

"None of this is going to make me look stupid, is it?" She definitely picked out things that felt kind of…different. And I've been instructed on how to properly wear my new clothes. I can't tuck my shirt in, my pants need to sit lower than I'm used to, and there isn't much material to my socks.

"Never," she says. "I made sure you look very nice, which isn't that hard to do." Her smile instantly brings one to my face too.

"So since I have no memory and can't tell you anything about me, why don't you tell me something about you?"

She shrugs. "What do you want to know?"

"I mean, I'm not even positive what it is that you do at the lab."

"Oh, I'm a biomedical researcher," she explains. "And Perry is a medical technology researcher—he likes gadgets, not blood. Anyway, we work together to create new biotechnology."

I give her a blank stare and she elaborates. "Basically, we try to come up with ways to help people with medical conditions. Typically with devices and other equipment."

"Oh okay. Very cool."

She smiles. "Yeah, it's nice when we develop something that really makes a difference. I didn't realize that the job came with a lot of paperwork for funding, though. Good thing River Valley's been fully funding us so far."

"That's good. You must've gone through a lot of schooling then, right?" I push what's left of my melted ice cream aside.

"Yeah. I'm from Olympia, so I went to Olympia Medical School. I stayed with family, so I was able to save money while going to school."

"What about what you do for fun?"

"Fun?" she asks with a smirk. "What's that?"

"That busy, huh?" I doubt my sudden appearance helped at all.

Chapter Six

"Well, yeah, but it's more just that the responsibilities have been building so much and there's just not enough time anymore to do everything, you know?"

I put up a hand. "Currently fresh out of responsibilities."

"That you know of."

"True."

"No, when I first moved out here I used to love hiking the mountains," she says. "Actually, it's what drew me to Ellsworth to begin with. The views. The valley. It's all so beautiful. Especially when it snows."

"What made you stop?"

"I was working on a big project with EIT and EMG at the hospitals downtown that had me working long hours. By time I finished, the weather had shifted and it wasn't safe to hike with the snow and ice. Once it broke, I just got used to not doing it, you know?"

"I could see that. But you kind of lost me with those acronyms."

She giggles. "Oh, EIT is Ellsworth Institute of Technology. They're probably the most prestigious university here in the city, but the Ellsworth Medical College is right up there with it. And EMG stands for Ellsworth Medical Group, which mostly consists of the three downtown hospitals: Ellsworth General, Ellsworth Children's, and Ellsworth Cancer. It's also an umbrella group for several other doctors' offices and stuff, but it's mainly those three hospitals on the medical campus down there."

"Okay then," I say with a grin. "You sound like a very intelligent person and I really think you should get out and hike more."

She laughs. "Yeah, I should go. Especially now that it's warm again. But we also suddenly just got a new specimen to research." She smirks.

"And I appreciate all of the work you're doing into it," I say. "But the mountains are beautiful. Well, the eastern mountain is beautiful. The western one—"

"The one you woke up in?"

I nod. "Yeah. That one still gives me the creeps. I'd rather not go back there, if I can help it."

"Does it bring back bad memories?"

"Not especially, just…bad feelings, you know?"

She nods, lost in thought. "Interesting. I'm sure I'll have more questions later, but I won't bombard you with them tonight." She laughs again. "It's your night off."

In a flash, I'm struck with another painful headache like the one I had yesterday when the Gatekeeper first arrived. This time, though, my vision shows me sitting at a table like this one, across from a beautiful girl with her dirty blonde hair held back by a headband. She smiles and takes my hand, intertwining her fingers with mine.

Her mouth moves as she talks, but I can't hear what she's saying. Instead, I just feel a burning sensation in the pit of my stomach and complete happiness. This woman is—or was—someone special.

"Ash!" Rachel's shaking my shoulder, forcing me out of it. "Are you okay?"

Slowly, I sit back and take a deep breath. The food in my belly suddenly feels like it's about to make an encore appearance, but I keep it down. Now that I'm no longer immersed in the vision, I feel a sense of longing, almost like homesickness.

"What's going on with you?" she asks.

I shake my head. "I don't really know."

"Let's get out of here." She comes around behind me and tucks her hands in my armpits, lifting until she brings me to my feet.

"I'm okay."

"Are you sure?"

I nod. "Now I am."

She grabs my bags.

"I can get those."

Chapter Six

"No," she tells me. "Let's go back to the car. We need to get you back to Vernon's. You should get some sleep. We'll talk in the morning."

The vision, albeit short, has taken its toll. I feel weaker, more tired. So I don't complain when Rachel ushers me out to the parking lot.

In the car, we don't say anything as she makes her way back into the city. She takes an exit out of the underground expressway and suddenly we're in a quiet residential neighborhood.

The whole place feels incredibly familiar to me. The quiet, tree-lined street next to the river. The view of the mountains. The moon high in the sky.

I wonder if this is where I'm from. If this is where I lived before I lost my memories. Is my family sitting in one of these houses we pass by, worried that I'm not home, completely unaware that I'm right outside? Or that girl? What is she doing to find me? *Is* she doing anything?

Rachel slams on the brakes and I throw my hands on the dash to keep myself steady.

"What the hell?" I shout, but follow her gaze through the windshield.

There's someone standing in the middle of the street. It's a man, I think. Someone large, for sure. Height and build. He just stands there. I wonder if something's wrong.

"Stay here," I tell Rachel.

"Wait!" she says, but I'm already out of the car.

"Are you okay?" I call out, standing behind the open door for protection.

He doesn't say anything, only takes a step forward with loud screeches as he moves. Like a rusted car door opening, but more piercing. My eyes adjust in the darkness and I notice more features about him. His body isn't just large, it's misshapen, bulkier than any normal person usually is.

Coming around the door carefully, I take a step closer.

"Ash! What are you doing?" Rachel shouts from the driver's seat.

I put my hand out to silence her, but keep my eyes on the misshapen man. He moves again and the glow from a nearby streetlight reflects off of him. He's wearing something metallic, but I can't make out exactly what *it* is.

I decide to keep my distance and not move any further. "Are you okay?" I ask again, louder this time.

He takes one step closer and the front of Rachel's car begins to shake.

In the time it takes for me to judge the distance to Rachel's side of the car and the time it would take to get her away from it, the license plate rips off the front and sticks to the man's chest.

"What the hell was that?" Rachel shouts from behind the wheel, but I simply stare at the man.

The sound of screeching metal intensifies as the man charges toward me. He extends his arm and opens his hand, which sends pieces of metal fragments flying my way.

I dive to the pavement, scuffing the palms of my hands. When I turn, the man is facing me, but staggering backward toward Rachel's car, as if he's about to fall.

Raising my bloody palms up, I allow the strength I felt last night to flow through me and shoot a single fireball at the center of his chest.

Dead hit.

The metal in the middle of his chest where my attack hit slides to the street, revealing a charred button-down shirt beneath. I need to be careful, otherwise I might seriously hurt this man.

When he regains his footing, the metal quickly slides back up his body and reattaches itself in place, like a suit of armor. Now that I've made the first move, the man charges toward me and I run to put distance between us and Rachel.

One block over, the river winds closer to the street, away

Chapter Six

from the quiet houses that tickle my memory.

A piece of metal flies past my head. I whip around to face him, igniting my hands and swinging them in the air in an effort to catch him off guard. A warning to stay back.

It doesn't discourage him and he charges at me with heavy footsteps. Nervously, I wait until he's close and then sink to the ground, holding out my leg to trip him. Only, it doesn't work the way I want it to. Instead, the man blows through, spinning me on the ground, and sending pain shooting up my leg.

Shit, I hope it's not broken.

Carefully, I get to my feet. My leg holds up. It's sore, but definitely not broken. Bruised beyond belief, probably.

The man recovers and turns back to me. Closer—too close. This time, I feel myself being pulled in his direction from my waistline.

My belt.

Quickly, I fumble with the buckle and unfasten it before I'm stuck to him. With my pants a little looser, I put more space between us by running backward a few steps.

He seems just as surprised as I am that my belt is now clinging to him from the buckle. His pause gives me time to raise my hands again and fire a steady stream of flame in his direction. It hits him so hard that he flies backward, tripping over the cobblestone fence on his way down to the river, knocking rocks and mortar off onto the sidewalk.

Shit, definitely not what I wanted to do.

I race toward the busted fence and scan the water. No sign of him. I can't let him drown like that. I need to get him out. There's a small strip on the other side of the fence before the edge of the water. I hop over, ignite a ball of flame in my palm for light and look around.

Nothing.

Jumping the fence, I follow the river downstream, looking for any sign of him. Maybe the choppy water carried him down, but he managed to grab onto something to stop him from floating further. Or maybe he only rolled down to the edge of the water and decided to run before he got hit with another one of my attacks.

Hopefully.

Rachel pulls up on the street and shouts from the driver's seat.

"Ash, you're a moron!"

"I can't find him," I say.

"He attacked you, why would you look for him?"

"In case he got hurt."

"Just get in the car! I'm taking you back."

Sweeping the area one more time, I finally concede and head back to the car. I hope I didn't kill him, or send him off to his death.

Chapter Seven

Thump thump thump.

I spread out and stretch, feeling every muscle in my body tighten and ache as I move.

Thump thump thump.

The door.

Where am I? Don't tell me this memory wipe is an everyday thing. I mean, at least I remember my dream. Not that it was a good one. Two people screaming for help as they were burned alive. Not the best way to welcome in the morning. At least it's over and I'm…here. Somewhere.

Vernon's house. Yes, that's where I am.

I pull my head out from under the covers and am immediately blinded by the morning light streaming in the window. I forgot to close the curtains last night.

Thump thump thump.

"Yeah?" I croak in my morning voice. Still better than my cave voice.

"Phone call," a small foreign voice says from the other side of the door.

"Just a minute." I toss the covers aside and hang my feet over the edge of the bed. I'm exhausted and refreshed all in one. I need food and a shower and maybe then I'll feel better. My palms still ache from meeting the pavement last night and the muscle in my leg feel tight. I wonder if I'll be able to just walk it off.

The jeans I wore from the store yesterday lay on a chair in the corner. I limp over, pull them on, and open the door. A Hispanic woman is on the other side—is this Rosa?—holding one of those weird-looking flat box phones to her ear.

"Sorry to wake you, sir, but Miss Chandler insisted on speaking with you," she says.

Miss Chandler? Who the hell is that?

"It's okay," I tell her.

She hands me the phone and I put it to my face—hoping it's the right way.

"Hello?" I close the door and stagger back to sit on the bed.

"Ash, it's Rachel. I need you to come down to ESTR today."

I rub the sleep out of my eyes. "Why?"

"I woke up thinking about what happened yesterday."

"Which part?"

"That weird headache thing you got at the mall."

"Oh." The vision of the girl. I dreamt of her a bit last night, but she also morphed into Rachel halfway through, so I'm not sure it was so much a memory as much as it was a fantasy. Definitely keeping that bit to myself.

"*And*," she goes on, "I think we should try to identify Black Magnet."

"*Black Magnet*?" I chortle.

"Look, if Perry can come up with names, then so can I."

"Okay."

"He was definitely magnetically charged somehow," she adds. "Thanks to him, I need to get a new front license plate."

Chapter Seven

"Good luck explaining that one."

"Yeah. So are you coming?"

"I'll be there," I say. "I just need to shower and eat...and find a ride down."

"Give me a call if you can't find someone to drop you off. You got a pen to write down my number?"

I spot one on the dresser and scribble it out on the back of a receipt from one of the bags.

"Got it."

"Keep that number," she tells me. "Call me if you need anything, okay?"

"Okay."

"See you later."

After I hang up, I head to the bathroom, turn the faucet on and take a shower. Even though I've showered here before, nothing quite compares to the massage jet shower heads—*plural*—that help relieve the knots in my shoulders. The soap stings as it runs all over the newest scrapes on my palms, but it's easy enough to forget.

After about ten minutes of standing under the hot water, I finally get out and towel off, stepping back into the bedroom to dig through my bags of new clothes for something to wear. My leg feels better, but I still baby it by taking careful steps. Just another reminder that even if I am somehow fireproof, I'm still breakable. I pull on khaki shorts, a white T-shirt, and a pair of bright red sneakers and head downstairs.

Daniela sits at the kitchen table that overlooks the flower garden beside the carriage house garage. I barely noticed it when I first arrived, but Vernon gave me a tour of it yesterday before we explored the city.

"Morning." I take a seat next to Vernon's wife.

Within seconds, Rosa sets a glass of water in front of me. "What else would you like to drink, sir? Coffee? Orange juice? Tea?"

I reach for the glass in front of me. "Water's fine for now, but I could use something to eat if you don't mind."

She smiles. "Certainly. I'll get started."

"Thank you," I say, but she's already behind the counter, whipping something up.

I turn back to Daniela and she offers a polite smile over her coffee. She's wearing a red floral sun dress and her long dark hair is braided down her back. "Did you sleep well?"

"I did, yes."

"Did you and Vernon have a good time last night?"

I scrunch my forehead. "Last night? I was with Rachel last night. She took me to the mall."

Daniela mimics my confusion. "My husband said *he* was taking you to the mall..."

I shake my head. "He wasn't there. It was just the two of us."

"Here we are," Rosa says cheerfully as she sets a plate of French toast and sausage links in front of me. "I hope you don't mind I gave you what was left from Mrs. Michaels' breakfast. If you want something else I can—"

"No, Rosa, it's fine. Thank you—"

"Oh, and here's your syrup." She pulls a bottle out of her apron pocket and sets it in front of the plate. "Anything else I can get for you?"

"No, thank you. This looks delicious."

"Enjoy." She disappears behind me and a moment later, I hear the clatter of the dishes as she begins to wash them.

The noise must aid in Daniela's confidence to ask more questions. She lowers her voice and says, "Vernon was gone all last night."

I shrug my shoulders and dig into my breakfast. "I don't know where he went."

She pulls out her phone and touches the screen several times and frowns after a minute.

"What's the matter?" I ask.

Chapter Seven

"My family app says he's here."

"Your family app?"

"Yeah, it shows where everyone in the family is—well, where their phones are."

I pull out the phone Rachel called and set it on the table. "Is this his phone?"

She takes it and looks it over, offering another frown. "One of them, yeah."

I swallow a bite of toast. "He has more than one?"

"Yeah." She sets the phone down on the table. "Personal and business."

"Oh."

"This is his personal one." She brings a hand to her mouth, looking as if she's about to cry.

"Mrs. Michaels, what's the matter?"

"I have no idea where he is," she says in an unusually high voice.

"You haven't heard from him?"

"Not since he left for work this morning." She sucks in a deep breath and looks out at the garden, trying to steady her voice. "Sometimes I wonder if he's having an affair."

"I'm sure that's not true," I say quickly, even though I have no way of knowing.

"I hope you're right." She sets her finished coffee mug on the table and rises to her feet. "If you see him, please let him know I'm looking for him."

"Will do."

"I'M HERE," I declare when I walk through the door into Perry and Rachel's lab. "I had to figure out the bus schedule, but I made it."

"Why didn't you just have Daniela or someone call you an

Uber?" Perry asks from his computer.

"A what?"

"Uber? Like the app?"

I nod slowly, still not getting it.

"Anyway," Rachel says to spare me the humiliation. She steps toward me from her desk, but notices my limp. "Are you okay? You're walking funny."

Perry snickers from his desk but she shuts him up by shooting him a look. The humor goes over my head and instead I look down at my leg.

"Just a small consequence of last night's activities," I say. "I'll be fine. It's already feeling better than it was."

"Good. And I'm glad you're here. We have some things we need to talk about."

Perry spins in his chair. "Yes, a lot of things."

"Theories, really," Rachel clarifies.

"Okay, so what is it?" I take a seat in one of the free chairs and cross my arms.

"Well, I think that headache you got last night was a flashback," she starts.

"I figured that much," I say.

"So I would like to do a scent test on you to see if we can trigger anymore memories that might help you remember who you are," she continues.

"A scent test?"

"The sense of smell has the strongest correlation to memory than any other sensory system," Perry clarifies.

"Based off of your lack of facial hair and there being no sign of long-term malnourishment, I'm willing to bet that you weren't in the cave for long," Rachel says. "So I think the likelihood of recovering those memories and finding where you belong is high."

Unconsciously, I run my hand over my chin. Only the faintest hint of stubble is there. I don't want to believe in Rachel's theories too quickly and get my hopes up, so I shoot them down in my head with other theories. Maybe I just don't grow facial hair very fast.

"That's good," I reply. "But it doesn't explain why I'm able to throw fire."

Perry puts up his hand. "That's another thing. We were both talking and we think it's probably a good idea if you practice those abilities."

"Really?" I smirk.

"Only so you don't accidentally hurt anyone with them," Rachel adds.

"Or in case you run into the Gatekeeper or—" he casts a sidelong glance at Rachel, "*Black Magnet* again."

Obviously, he's annoyed he didn't get to name that one.

"More like *when* I run into them again," I say. "I don't think either of them are going anywhere."

"Even more reason to practice," she says. "And I've been thinking about how you were able to fly when you went up against the Gatekeeper. You said you didn't know how you did it?"

I shake my head. "Not a clue."

"Well, I have a theory," she says. "I mean, it's just a thought. But when something is heated up, its density lowers, which alters the gravitational force on it."

"You think his body density is lowering as his body temperature rises?" Perry asks.

"Exactly," she says. "I mean, it's on a much larger scale, but it's the same idea."

"So the hotter I get, the higher I'm able to fly?"

"In theory."

Perry turns to me and smiles. "We'll just have to test that theory. And I have just the thing for it." He walks over to a cabinet on the other side of the room and pulls out a jumpsuit on a hanger. It's red leather, separated by a black section around the waist, wrists, and legs.

"What is it?" I step over and hold it out. There's a mask hanging from the hanger as well.

"This is your supersuit, so to speak," Perry announces. "It's so you no longer burn your clothes when you take flight."

"Are you still bitter about that?" Rachel asks with an eye roll.

"Yeah, those were my favorite pair of shorts!"

"Sorry," I murmur. "When did you come up with this?"

"Well, while you two were out buying clothes at the mall last night, I was busy making sure you wouldn't be arrested for public indecency."

I examine the mask. It has a built-in gas mask by the nose and mouth. I guess just in case I find myself covered in smoke. A black band covers the eyes as well.

"What's the mask for?" Rachel asks.

"To hide his identity," Perry says. "Can you imagine the scrutiny he'd be under if people knew his story?"

"But who's going to see him in this suit?" Rachel asks.

"Well, I'm sure there will be witnesses when he goes out and kicks ass with some of Ellsworth's criminals."

"You want me to play police officer with this?" I ask.

"Perry, that's not his job!" Rachel says. "We're supposed to be helping him remember who he is so he can get home. On top of that, we need to figure out why he's able to do what he does, not enabling him to be a superhero."

"Why can't we do both?" Perry asks. "How is Ash going out and nabbing some bad guys going to alter our research?"

"He could *die*, Perr, or get arrested," she says. "That's how."

"Guys," I cut in, but they ignore me.

"He's not going to die if they think he's a fire pit! Besides, the mask will cover his face, so no one will know who he is."

"Guys!" That stops them. "I agree that going after criminals has its risks, but you both said that you think I should practice my abilities in case Black Magnet comes back. And I think this might be the perfect way."

Chapter Seven

"Ash, you don't need to be a hero if you don't want to," Rachel says.

"You're right," I say. "But I have these abilities for a reason, right? Why not use them to help people? I mean, helping me remember who I am or why I'm able to do this mostly lies with you guys. You haven't come up with any new theories on that, have you?"

Rachel makes a face. "Well, it's quite obvious that your body has mutated somehow—for whatever reason. One of the most obvious causes of your pyrokinetics could be a house fire."

"Makes sense," I say.

"Yeah, but it didn't really pan out," Perry says.

I look between both of them. "What do you mean?"

"We looked through the fire department records of all the house fires in the last month and none of them listed any injuries of anyone matching your description," Rachel explains. "So we widened the search to any *structure* fire and there was a barn fire about half an hour outside of the city that sent a young man in his early twenties to the hospital. He was transferred to Ellsworth General downtown."

"You think that's me?" I ask.

"We did," Perry says. "But…he's still there and you're here, so obviously that's not the case."

"We even tried looking through missing person files, but it didn't come up with any results that I could find," she says. "But then, I'm not a detective. It might be a good idea to consider—"

"We're not taking him to the police," Perry says. "Not with what he can do. And besides, he's an adult. If he can't remember, they're going to put him in a psychiatric center or something."

"They wouldn't do that," she counters.

"But they're certainly not going to be able to help him any better than we can."

"You don't know that!"

"Guys, I don't want to go to the police," I cut them both off.

"Perry's right. I don't want to broadcast my abilities to everyone. Now, do you have any other leads to figure out who I am?"

Rachel shrugs. "Only try to get you to remember."

"Oh." My heart sinks a little bit. I didn't realize I was getting my hopes up for something to come of their efforts.

"We'll figure it out, Ash," she says.

We're quiet a moment. Rachel and Perry are limited in what they can do to find out who I am. Their focus is in the medical field, not detective work. Besides, this isn't their jobs. I need to do my part as well.

"Well, I think this just proves that there's even more reason for me to do what I can with my powers."

"Ash…" Rachel starts.

"No, listen. You can run your tests and put together theories, meanwhile all I can do is try to remember. That hasn't been working for me so far. Let me do something useful."

She crosses her arms and studies me. "You really want to do this?"

"I think it's the best use of my abilities for now," I say.

She turns to Perry. "How safe is this suit?"

He rocks his head back and forth. "Pretty safe. We can do a couple dry runs before he goes out, but I think he should be all set."

"Don't think. Make sure he is."

He nods.

"And Ash, you need to be careful."

"Are you giving me your blessing?" I ask.

She sighs heavily. "Yes."

"All right! Heat is back in business!" Perry exclaims.

We both look at him.

"Heat?" I ask.

He shrugs. "What? I just thought that if you had a cool new suit, you could have a cool new name to go along with it."

I rock my head back and forth. "That's not bad, actually."

Chapter Seven

"Either way, Ash needs some practice before he starts doing anything," Rachel says. "Get him into the field as soon as possible before you guys start coming up with excuses not to."

"Sure, you want to go now?" I ask.

Perry's computer starts making an alarm sound.

"What's that?" Rachel asks.

"It's an alert that notifies me when something's happening in the city," he explains. "Just installed it."

"For what?"

Perry motions to me and reads off his computer, "Armed robbery. Maple Avenue and Park Street." He looks up at me. "I don't think Heat's going to get any practice time in."

Chapter Eight

Consumed in flame, I land hard on the ground in the midst of the robbery. Rachel's theory was right. The hotter my fire burns, the higher I'm able to fly. And, with the new suit Perry created, I don't drop naked in the middle of a crime scene.

Bullets whiz by me and I duck for cover behind a parked car that sports plenty of holes already. The shooting stops for a moment, but picks up again shortly after I've taken cover.

Now protected behind my perch, I take in the scene. An armored car sits in front of a Bank of America. One guard shoots from inside. Two thugs flank the backside of the car while a third keeps the driver busy, shooting from a car parked in front of it. On the sidewalk between the armored car and the bank, I spot another guard bleeding out on the pavement.

I move to the back end of the car I'm hiding behind and eye up my shot. I don't know if I'm able to control the temperature of the flame I throw. I don't want to permanently hurt anyone, but

Chapter Eight

these men need to be stopped. Guess there's no way of knowing what I'm capable of until I do it.

Opening up my palm, I fire a quick stream of flame at the gunman flanking this side of the armored car. When the blast hits him, he's slammed against the side of the car and falls to the street unconscious.

Well, that's one down.

Gunshots hit the car that's keeping me covered. I've given away my location. Clearly, I'm not a Navy Seal.

The sound of gunfire intensifies. It must be that the second gunman is taking his turn on me. I wonder how impervious I am to bullets when I'm consumed in flame.

Only one way to find out.

Like a rocket, I shoot up into the sky, burning hotter than I think I ever have before—not that it's saying much since as far as I know I've only had these abilities for a few days.

Once I'm in the air and out of firing range of the men, I let my body cool and drop back down to the street, landing next to the second gunman at the back of the armored car.

He's stunned as the flame dissipates and I'm left standing unharmed. I knock the rifle out of his hands and drive a firm punch right to his face.

That hurts.

Out of the corner of my eye, I catch the gunman who was shooting at the guard taking off on foot down the street. A group of police officers chase him, but he manages to shoot one of them down as he runs. Sliding the gun behind his back, he jumps and catches hold of the fire escape ladder and climbs up.

My body bursts into flames again and I meet him on the roof, only he's not stunned like the man on the street was. He pulls his rifle to his front before I can reach him and fires.

I drop to the ground and send a stream of fire to his feet.

He jumps, but maintains his position.

In flames once again, I rise up into the air and shoot another stream of fire at him, but I miss and it strikes right next to an exhaust pipe. I need to be careful or I'm going to set this building on fire.

Rising higher above him, the gunman cranes his neck to keep his eyes on me, not watching his footing. He stumbles on the same exhaust pipe I nearly took out and falls to his butt.

Wasting no time, I shoot down to him, sending a fire stream ahead of me to knock his gun away. I let the flames dissipate a few feet from the roof and pounce on him, pushing him down on his stomach as police officers begin to flood in from the staircase.

Once they get ahold of him, I back off and let them do their job. One officer steps toward me and offers a thanks, but I don't reply—too scared that they might try to arrest me for interfering with a crime scene.

In a burst of flame, I take off into the sky.

VERNON IS WAITING with Rachel and Perry when I get back to ESTR. He's sitting at an empty desk playing on his phone, which he sets down when he sees me walk in in the Heat suit.

"What are you wearing?" he asks.

Perry's head snaps up and he rushes to me, ushering me in so he can close the door to their lab behind me. "Dude, are you insane? Don't let the other workers here see you in the Heat suit!"

"The Heat suit?" Vernon echoes.

"Why not?" I ask Perry.

"Secret identity, remember?"

"Since you didn't talk to the police, there's a chance that they'd look into any leads on your whereabouts," Rachel says. "It's probably a good idea to keep a low profile."

"Okay, but how did you know I didn't talk to them?" I ask.

"Live coverage from the scene," Vernon says. "It's how I knew to come here. I figured the human flamethrower was probably you and I figured these two would be involved."

Rachel puts up her hands in surrender. "Hey, the Heat suit was not my concoction, nor was it my idea to encourage Ash to go out and fight bad guys."

Perry smiles like a giddy kid at Christmas. "But it was pretty cool."

It's infectious, bringing an instant smile to my face too. "Yeah it was, wasn't it?"

"All right, boys, that's enough," Rachel says. She carries over a flat monitor to me. It almost looks like a larger version of those weird phones they all seem to have. "Thanks to the equipment Perry installed in the suit, I was able to take some readings while you were out there. Looks like I was right about the body heat and density theory."

I nod. "Yeah, I definitely noticed it too. It helped a lot with trying to maneuver around."

"Good. That's good," she says. "But you still need to be careful with those bullets. Your body temperature registered between six hundred and a thousand degrees Celsius, which is about the same temperature of a standard campfire."

"Really? That hot?" Vernon asks.

She nods. "Yeah, but even with that temperature, it's not enough to melt a passing bullet."

"Got it. Bullets bad."

"I'm being serious, Ash," she says. "If you're going to insist on going out and putting yourself in dangerous situations, you need to be aware of the consequences."

Perry waves a finger in her direction and shoots me a look. "It's a good idea to listen to her. She knows her stuff."

"Okay, I'll be more careful," I concede.

"And, I don't really like it that you're going in solo," she adds.

I shake my head. "No, I don't feel comfortable with anyone else jumping into those situations. I know my powers don't make me invincible, but they certainly help."

"I wasn't talking about giving you a sidekick," she says. "I think you need an earpiece so we can watch your back from here." She turns to Perry. "That's where you come in. You've developed the Heat suit—equipped with a gas mask—that can withstand those high temperatures. We need you to come up with a communication device that can do the same."

Perry makes a face. "I'm not sure any tech will be able to withstand that. Especially with the radio waves that it'd need to tap into to connect with us remotely. I'm not sure we'd be able to talk to him when he's operating at that temperature."

"But you need to try," she says. "As of right now, the only eyes we have on him is when the news does live coverage. That's not enough."

"Okay, I'll see what I can do," he says.

"Good. Thank you."

The room falls quiet. Perry focuses on his computer, likely already starting his research into the communication device. Rachel taps away at her portable monitor.

"Are we all set with the post-robbery checklist?" Vernon asks.

I cross the room and grab my clothes from the cabinet Perry had the Heat suit stored in.

Rachel motions up to the medic room. "You can change up there. Just pull the curtain closed."

I nod and head up the few steps into the medic room to change in private. Vernon's voice follows once I close the curtain. He's probably standing in the doorway between the two rooms.

"So I didn't just come here tonight to hang out," he starts.

I unzip the suit in the back and peel it off of me. I've been sweating and the leather feels tight. I should mention it to Perry. Maybe he can make some adjustments to make it more breathable.

"I'm having a dinner party at my house on Friday and I

Chapter Eight

would like to know if you all would like to come," Vernon announces. "It'll be you folks and several of my friends from work. You know, Lisa, Marge, Jerry, maybe even Robert. I figured it's a good way to remind my team—mostly my boss, Mr. Cain—how important the work is that you two do here."

"Really?" Rachel sounds surprised. She doesn't say anything else so I imagine she didn't mean to blurt it out.

I pull my street clothes on now that the Heat suit is laid out on the hospital bed beside me.

"Yeah, I think it'd be fun," Vernon says. "I also thought it'd be a good way to, uh, kind of *introduce* Ash to the world."

"But he *is* a part of this world," Perry says. "He's not an alien. He has a name—probably even has a last name. He just can't remember it."

"Have you guys gotten any closer to figuring that out?" he asks.

Silence.

"Well, in the meantime, Ash can enjoy life as just Ash," he goes on. "No last name. No prior obligations. No expectations. Even if he did drop down from space, on Friday he'll just be my houseguest."

"Are you sure your family's okay with that?" I ask, pushing the curtain aside now that I'm dressed. "Your wife didn't seem too thrilled when I first showed up. By the way, have you talked to her today?"

He nods. "I called her at lunch. I realized I forgot my phone after I left this morning."

I nod. "Right."

"Anyway, they'll be fine," he says. "Daniela even thinks it's a good idea. She loves dinner parties."

Judging by the looks on Rachel's and Perry's faces, they don't share her enthusiasm.

"Anyway, just think about it," he says. "It'll be fun."

"Uh, sure." I'm fresh out of reasons not to. Especially since

I've been staying there. If nothing else, I owe it to Vernon as a thank you for his hospitality. Even if he was hesitant to offer it at first.

"Great!" he says. "It'll be Friday at my house at six. Formal attire, of course. Please let me know if any of you would like to bring a guest."

Perry puts up a finger. "Just me."

"And me," I add. "Well, obviously."

Rachel glances at me and then at Vernon. "I'll let you know."

Who could she be bringing?

"Fantastic!" He smiles wide. "I'll let Rosa know so she can have enough food prepared."

Well, this makes him happy. And I'm glad to see that. I'm just nervous about all the questions I'll inevitably get at the party.

"OKAY, THE FIRST round is up." Perry carries three bottles of beer over to our high-top table.

"*First* round?" Rachel asks. "Perry, we have to work tomorrow."

"All right, *Mom*. We're grown adults. We can handle breaking from our usual evening routine once in a while."

She shoots him a look. "I have a life, you know."

"Oh really?" He takes a sip. "Could've fooled me. What *exactly* did you do last night?"

"Took Ash shopping."

"And you were home by, what, eight o'clock?"

"That doesn't mean anything."

As both of them banter back and forth about going out on a Tuesday night, I take in the room. We're at a small bar—The Troll's Hideout—on Bridge Street on the outskirts of downtown. Perry thought we could all use a night off to relax and forget about work and Heat stuff and just have fun.

Chapter Eight

Rachel glances down at her phone. "I wanna be home by seven."

"You can do whatever you want," he tells her. "But you're not really giving Ash here a warm welcome."

"I saved his life," she counters.

"And where did he wake up? On a *cold* table in a *cold* medic room."

"He throws fire."

"Guys," I interrupt them with a laugh. "It's okay. I don't mind. It's not like I have any other plans anyway."

"See? He's more pathetic than I am!" Rachel snickers.

Perry raises his bottle. "No, but seriously, I just want to officially welcome Ash to our psychotic, demented family."

"Psychotic?" Rachel asks.

"Demented?" I echo.

"We're weird, all right," he says. "Just clink the damn bottles and let's move on."

We laugh and raise our glasses and each take a sip.

"I'm guessing if you two consider yourselves family that you've been working together a while, right?"

Rachel shakes her head. "We don't really consider each other family. I mean, not in the traditional sense. Well, I guess you could say it's our *work* family, but it's really just the two of us and that just seems…" She trails off and glances at her phone.

"We're like brother and sister," Perry clarifies. "She didn't like me when we met."

She cocks her head. "Oh, like I was *your* favorite person back then."

"We had a bit of a rough start," Perry tells me.

"Is this when you started at the lab?"

Rachel shakes her head. "No, we first met when we were working on a project that was a collaboration between the Ellsworth Medical Group and the Ellsworth Institute of Technology."

"It was a temporary grant that was paying our bills that year," Perry adds.

"Neither of us had steady full-time work up until that point," she explains.

"It was always about taking temporary jobs in order to gain experience in the hopes that we'd land a better gig," he says.

"Sounds stressful," I say.

"Oh, it was," he says.

"Which is why when River Valley Holdings announced it was providing funding for a lab that would study ways to improve the quality of life, specifically in the medical technology field, we both jumped at it."

Perry rolls his eyes. "All right, *Professor*. At that point in my life, I was mostly concerned with paying my rent."

"Oh please," she counters. "You and I both know that's not true. You like being able to help people."

He grins. "Anyway, when River Valley announced its funding, neither of us thought we had strong enough proposals on our own so even though we weren't the biggest fans of each other, we presented a joint proposal. Now here we are!"

"We've since grown on each other," she adds.

"I can see that," I say with a chuckle. "What didn't you guys like about each other?"

"Well, Miss Priss over here was a giant stick in the mud," he starts.

"And you were very sloppy," she counters.

"So you both kind of rubbed off on each other?"

They both turn away and grumble an acknowledgment.

"Well, I'm glad you two are friends now," I say. "Seriously, I don't know what I would've done if you hadn't—"

Perry holds up a hand and turns away. "Nope! We're not talking about Heat stuff tonight!"

"Shh," Rachel warns.

He looks around. "Nobody's listening. And nobody knows!"

Chapter Eight

"Perry's right," Rachel concedes. "Let's talk about something else."

"Uh...I don't know," I stammer. "What was college like?"

I can't remember if I've ever been to college. I don't want to voice that, though, because I'm afraid that falls under the "Heat" category. Best to let them talk.

"Oh," Rachel says with a grin. "College was fun."

"*Really*?" Perry asks, shocked. "Did you write in your textbooks? Turn an assignment in late? Stayed up on a school night?"

She shoots him another look. "It doesn't need to be a school night to get the *full* college experience."

"Hoo-hoo-hoo!" He hops in place. "You were a party girl?"

She smiles. "I mean, my undergrad *was* practically downtown."

"Where was your undergrad?" I ask.

"Olympia University," she says. "I grew up out there before moving here. I went to Olympia Medical School for my advanced degrees."

"Wait, no," Perry interrupts. "No, no, no, no, no. You are not getting off the hook with this whole party girl thing. You've been holding out on me!"

"Okay, Perry, you're exaggerating," she says. "I wasn't like table dancing and meeting random guys for hookups."

"I didn't say you were doing *that*."

"It was just...a few parties." She shrugs and winks at me.

"How often?" he pushes.

"It doesn't matter," she says. "That was several years ago."

"All right, that's it! I'm getting shots." He makes his way back over to the bar.

"Wait, Perry, no!" she calls after him, but he ignores her. Turning back to me, she sighs. "Fine. I guess one shot can't hurt."

"So...party girl, huh?" I ask.

She scrunches her face. "Yeah. I had a bit of a wild streak. Nothing too crazy, but I knew I was going to medical school and

I knew once I had classes there, I wouldn't have any time for parties so I wanted to make the most of it. Obviously, I've changed a lot since then."

I shake my head. "No, I think you still have a bit of a wild side."

"How so?"

"I can just tell."

"Like you're one to talk, Mr. Stopped-An-Armed-Robbery."

"I believe our friend has deemed that topic off-limits for tonight," I say.

She glances back at Perry as the bartender sets three shot glasses in front of him. "What he doesn't know won't hurt him."

"Well, before he comes back, I just want to say that I'm glad we all met."

"Hey, you're one of us now," she says. "We're friends."

Friends. I like that.

"All right, here we go!" Perry returns, balancing all three glasses between his fingers. "Drink up!"

Chapter Nine

"Ready?" Rachel asks as she backs down Vernon's driveway. Since I don't have a ride to ESTR and Rachel and Perry want to run more tests on me, she offered to give me a ride in on her way to work each morning. Of course, that means getting up in time for her eight o'clock pickup time. After last night's activities, that was harder than I expected.

"All set," I say once I'm buckled.

She pulls onto the street and heads downtown toward one of the only three bridges in the city that crosses the Percival River. Learned that on my excursion with Vernon the other day.

"How's it going at the Michaels'?" she asks.

"It's all right, I guess."

"Still kind of weird?"

"Yeah, a bit," I say. "I tried to get a feel for what the rest of his family thought of the dinner party Vernon's having, but nobody really said anything. Everybody basically keeps to themselves."

She nods. "They're kind of all private people...even with

each other. It's weird."

"So I take it it's not normal for Vernon to have dinner parties?"

"No, it is. He usually has at least one company gathering a year, but Perry and I aren't always invited."

"Why's that?"

She shrugs. "More important people to invite, I guess. People with money."

"Ah, I got it."

"Yeah. But it should be fun. We'll protect you from the crazies."

I laugh. "Thanks. But it seemed like he was having this party for me."

"You?"

"Yeah. I don't know. I mean, it was really sudden, and he's inviting all his work friends. I don't know, maybe I'm just reading into it, but it just seems…"

"Weird?"

"That's a really good word to describe him, isn't it?" I ask with a chuckle.

She shrugs again. "He's probably just trying to connect with you somehow. Me, you, and Perry have hit it off pretty well. Maybe he's just feeling left out."

"Maybe."

It would help if I knew if I was the type of person who *liked* going to dinner parties and hanging out with people outside of my social class. Well, that's assuming they *are* outside my social class. Maybe I'm actually part of the upper class. Doubtful, but maybe.

When we get to the lab, Perry's at his work table with his back to us soldering something in front of him.

"What are you working on?" Rachel asks as she steps over to her desk.

He pushes his safety glasses up into his curly hair and

straightens his eyeglasses. "I came in early to work on that communication device that you wanted for Ash."

"How's it coming?" I ask.

"We'll see how it stands up to a flamethrower." He smiles wide, like a devious little kid.

"I'm assuming you have a very controlled environment to test this?" Rachel asks.

He shakes his head. "Ash isn't going to be in a controlled environment when he's out in the field. He's going to be facing unpredictable circumstances and this device needs to hold up."

She sighs, not offering any other criticism.

"Besides," he adds, "that's not even the worst part. I need to make sure the frequency doesn't make him go deaf with the changing altitudes and pressure when he goes full on burning man."

I reach for my ear. "No, I'd like to keep my hearing."

"That's the plan." He shifts his safety glasses back on and returns to work.

I join Rachel over at her desk. "What tests are you running today?"

"Well," she starts with a sigh, "I have a report I need to get done for this Pellman project and I have to check in on some of my other ongoing projects. So, unfortunately, you kind of take a backseat to the stuff that pays my mortgage."

Can't blame her there.

"Luckily, there's something you can do on your own." She crosses the room to the cabinet next to the one Perry pulled my Heat suit out of yesterday. "It's in here somewhere..." She digs through the cabinet, shifting around vials, needles, gloves, and other biomedical supplies until she snatches up a box. "Ah, here it is!"

Carrying it over to an open work table, she pulls out a white package with tiny pockets and little tabs wedged in.

"You remember how I was telling you I wanted you to do a

scent test? Well, here are some common scents."

I scrunch my brow. "You want me to sniff stuff all day?"

"Well, not *all day*. Take your time with each of them. Soak it in, so to speak, try to access your deepest memories. Pick up on what's familiar and linger on that. If something smells—I don't know—comforting, stick with it for a bit to see if the lingering scent helps you remember anything."

Looking down at the package, I note how many tabs there are. Easily a hundred, maybe more.

"I'll do my best," I say.

"Let us know if you remember anything."

"I'll try, but I'll probably just end up desensitizing my nose. Hey, if Perry's device backfires, maybe I'll lose two senses in one day!"

He shoots me a look over his glasses.

"You'll be fine," Rachel says. "If you need to take a break, then go for a walk."

She settles into her desk and gets started on her work, so I get started on mine. Some of the scents are fairly common: Strawberries, vanilla, chocolate. Others are more specific: pepperoni pizza, something that smells like a musty basement, even wet pavement. Initially, none of them give me any sort of specific memory, even if they all smell familiar. But, trusting Rachel I continue on.

All three of us work relatively quietly for the rest of the morning. Perry and I head over to West Side Pizza for lunch while Rachel stays in and continues on her paperwork, munching on the lunch she brought from home.

In the afternoon, with my hands freshly washed and the scent of pizza a memory, I dive back into the scent test. None of them seem to do much to trigger any sort of useful memory.

One of the tabs smelled like cherry chapstick, which reminded me of putting some on during the winter. Not a specific instance, just a regular habit. I wonder if she can get more unique scents to try to help. But then, in a world of infinite smells, finding the right ones that'll kickstart *my* memory is like finding a needle in a haystack.

By the end of the day I'm frustrated. Luckily, though, Vernon arrives just after four and since Perry and Rachel are still too busy working to talk, we decide to head out.

"Anything interesting happen today?" Vernon asks on the ride back to his house.

I lean my head against the back of the seat and study the car in front of us. Traffic is at a standstill to get across the bridge downtown.

"Not really," I tell him. "It's just been a long day."

"You'll get there eventually," he says.

"Maybe. It's just frustrating to spend all day trying to remember something that might not even be in my head anymore."

"They have you trying to recall memories?"

"Yeah."

"I'm sure it's still in there," he says. "But maybe the reason you've blocked them out is still too much for your psyche to take."

I consider that. I didn't think that I was blocking something out intentionally. All this time, I've been under the impression that something physical happened to me that caused the blockage.

Back at the Michaels', Rosa has dinner ready for us by time we get home. Even though the whole family is here, it's a pretty quiet meal. I wonder if it's always like this or if I'm the elephant in the room keeping conversation to a minimum. The food's good, though, so that helps.

After dinner, Vernon suggests I watch TV with his kids, but I'd rather not have to put on an act when I'm this exhausted. Not to mention, I'm the guest in their house. I don't want them to feel uncomfortable by my presence.

Instead, I spend the rest of the evening in my room reading

a book I pulled from the bookshelf in the hallway. It's a murder mystery. Maybe it'll get me to think outside the box to help with my own situation.

The next few days go by more or less the same. Rachel takes me to ESTR in the morning, I work on some memory tests—scents, scenes, sounds—and then Vernon takes me back to his house for a quiet meal with the family. After dinner, Perry picks me up and we head out to an open field outside the city to work on my abilities. It's helping me become more familiar with them, which will be helpful the next time I need to use them.

By Friday, when Rachel picks me up in the morning from Vernon's—just as she's done all week—we head down to ESTR on the west side of the city. It's dinner party day, as Rachel has so wonderfully reminded me. I was hoping it would somehow disappear, but nonetheless I suppose I owe it to Vernon since he's taken me in. At least I have a full day to get my mind off of it before I need to get ready.

When we get into Lab #8, though, the alert on Perry's computer rings out loudly.

"There's a high-speed chase downtown," Perry tells me.

My heart races with fear, but still I rush over to the cabinet and grab my Heat suit.

Within minutes, I'm out the door and shooting into the air in a mass of flames toward downtown. Perry didn't give me concrete directions, but a high-speed chase shouldn't be hard to find.

I'm still working on speed control, which is obvious when I go to slow down. The fire covering me spurts out and I start to drop.

And panic.

I ignite once more and shoot higher into the sky. After somersaulting in the air for a bit, I regain control. Once I'm steady again, I catch sight of the chase and zoom forward.

Hovering over the leading car—a black SUV—I speed up enough so when I cut the firepower, I'll be able to grab on. I sink lower, but as we move out of downtown and into the residential section, I smack into tree branches and I'm forced to rise higher.

I wait for another break in the trees and then dive toward the car again, letting my temperature cool so my body sinks until I slam onto the top of the vehicle. My hands grip the cross bars on the roof, but still the momentum makes it hard to keep my grip.

Struggling to hang on as the driver meanders the vehicle around the growing morning rush hour traffic, I finally get a second to breathe when there's a clear shot on the street. With my body shaking from nerves, I reach around and place my hand on the driver's window, releasing a trickle of increasing heat until the glass shatters.

"Son of a bitch!" a man's voice from below calls out.

Gunshots fire and I pull my hand away, but not quick enough. Scorching pain shoots up my arm. Hooking my feet against the cross bars on the roof to support me, I clutch my injured hand with my free one.

Bad timing.

The vehicle makes a sharp left and I'm thrown off in the opposite direction. I hit the pavement hard, luckily not cracking my skull. A pair of empty garbage bins on the sidewalk break the rest of my fall.

My back pops as I get to my feet. Trying my best to ignore the pain, I quickly charge toward them on foot, eventually encompassing myself in flame again to speed up my pursuit. On the way up, I smack into a couple branches, but the fire that surrounds me helps soften the blow. Since the trees are green, I don't have to worry about them catching fire too easily.

Once free of obstructions, it takes me a minute to locate the SUV. The screams of bystanders help direct me, though. I fire a single attack down at the vehicle, hitting the roof but not causing any significant damage. The car continues to speed through the city.

I fire another attack, this time aiming for in front of the

vehicle. They swerve to dodge it, but the front right tire still catches part of the flame. There's a loud *pop*, and the car squeals to a stop, only a few feet from a large oak tree.

Dropping to the ground—this time much more gracefully—I rush to the car, opening the door and grabbing the driver. He reaches for a handgun and fires. The shot whizzes by my ear and I grab his hand, pointing the gun up as I let heat trickle out until he's forced to drop the gun.

Meanwhile, his passenger takes off at a sprint down the sidewalk. Still clutching the driver, I extend my free arm and shoot flame at the passenger, hitting him square in the back and knocking him to the ground. I hear sirens in the distance. The police will be here soon.

Job well done, Heat, I think to myself.

The driver squirms and manages to break free of my grasp. I run to catch up to him, but he's quick. I follow him over fences, across private backyards, and even through traffic. If I tried to fly to catch up to him, I would likely lose him with the tree cover or start something on fire when I dove after him. Best to stay on foot.

I trail him all the way to the industrial part of town, where he jumps a rusted chain-linked fence blocking off what appears to be an abandoned plant. Forgotten box trucks beyond repair sit near an old loading bay. Weeds and grass grow tall in the cracks in the pavement and around the trucks.

The man I've been chasing stops in the middle of the empty parking lot and my suspicions increase.

This is a set up.

I don't have time to react before the gunshots start. I dive behind a rusted old car for cover, trying to consider my next move.

I wish I had a way to communicate with Perry and Rachel. They might be able to offer better solutions.

Peeking over the hood of the car, I try to gauge where the gunshots are coming from without getting my head blown off.

Chapter Nine

The man I followed here is ducked next to an abandoned box truck by one of the loading bays. Shots fire out from two trucks over, so there's another man there. I can hear shots ring out to my left, but the rest of the car I'm hiding behind is in my line of view.

A bullet bounces off the hood only a foot away from where my head is and I slink back down to the cracked pavement. With three of them, there's no way in hell I'll be able to get a shot out without getting hit myself. I give half a thought to bursting into flame and shooting up into the air, but Rachel said the fire wouldn't stop the bullets. It's definitely not the time to test that theory.

Dropping further to the ground, I eye up my attackers from beneath the car, extend my arm as far as it will go underneath, and release a stream of flame at the attacker I chased here. His clothes catch fire as he drops and the man to the left runs to his aid to pat out the flames.

I fire again, knocking that one down as well, also igniting his clothes. The last one takes off into the building and I jump to my feet and run from my hiding place toward the men I just attacked.

I pat out the flames, check their pulses to make sure they're both still alive, and follow the last attacker into the plant through a broken side door to the right of the building.

Despite the morning sunshine outside, inside its dark. Many of the windows are boarded up and the ones that aren't are covered in years' worth of grime, which obscures the light.

Listening carefully for footsteps, I look around for any sign of the attacker. The plant is a big cavernous space with large metal beams holding the brick building up. Most of the equipment has been emptied out, leaving clear sight lines throughout the space.

Still, it smells like an old fireplace in here. The walls and floor are coated in what appears to be black soot and I spot dust particles floating in the sunlight streaming through a broken window. Good thing I have a mask to filter out these toxins.

I don't see the attacker, but along the opposite wall are offices—well, former offices. He must be hiding in there.

One step forward and I'm struck with intense pain between my eyes. Again.

I feel the hard flooring as I fall, but my mind takes me somewhere else entirely. I see my feet moving quickly along a rocky surface. I'm running. Fast. Soon, my footsteps are obscured by a black cloud until the vision fades into darkness and I wake up on the floor of the old plant, lying in soot.

I rise to my knees and try to make sense of what I just saw. Even though I only caught a glimpse of the place, I recognize it as the cave. A chill emanates from my core at the thought of it. Something bad happened in there. In the vision, though, I was running *into* it.

But why? And what was that black stuff? Was it smoke? Or was it simply my recollection of that scene fading?

The sound of gunfire brings me back to reality. The shot hits just in front of me, the shrapnel bouncing up against my chest. I dive behind one of the beams supporting the ceiling, knowing full-well that it doesn't completely conceal my body, but it's better than nothing.

Luckily, the attacker doesn't seem to be a good shot. Either that, or he's not trying to kill me.

Four more shots hit around me, with a fifth bouncing off the opposite side of the beam I'm hiding behind. Guess even bad shots get lucky once in a while.

I need to fend him off long enough to get closer. Throwing my arm toward him—chancing another bullet wound—I launch a fireball back toward the offices.

The building explodes in a rush of flame, knocking me backward. Within seconds, the whole building is engulfed and black smoke fills the room. The heat is nearly unbearable, even for me.

Chapter Nine

I wonder if it would be easier if I burst into flame myself, maybe my body could withstand it better. But I decide not to chance it. I already created this inferno as it is. I don't need to spread it.

Springing to my feet, I sprint through the fire to the other side of the building. If I'm having a hard time with this heat and the smoke, the unprotected attacker is in serious danger.

In the office, I try to look for him, but I can't see a thing. The way the fire spread everywhere tells me that it *was* soot on the floor and I'm the idiot who brought in the fire. The soot on the floor is what's ignited, meaning I can't drop to my knees to see under the smoke.

"Are you in here?" I call out to no answer. I wonder if he's dead. I don't want to think about the fact that I'm the reason.

The room isn't very large and I walk around a bit, feeling the sweat run down my back under the suit. I kick something and immediately drop down to feel what it is.

The man. His clothes are burning and he's not moving. Hauling him up over my shoulder, I press my hand against the grime-filled window and expel a quick burst of flame to break the glass. The flames behind me surge higher with the fresh air, and I do my best to ignore it and work on our escape.

Clearing some of the remnants away from the edge of the window, I drag the man over and slowly lower him down the side. We're only a few feet from the ground. Once he's out, I jump out behind him, and pat out the flames on his clothes. Watching the flames lick the side of the building out the window, I throw my attacker over my shoulder, and take off in a sprint back to the empty parking lot.

The other two attackers are gone. They probably took off after the explosion. I lay the man down on the pavement and check for a pulse.

It's weak, but it's there. I shake him, try to get him to wake up. After a minute, he gasps for air, but doesn't open his eyes. Still, relief washes over me and I lean back, noting the sound of sirens in the distance. Is that the fire department or is that still from the chase downtown? It's been a long day already and I haven't even had lunch yet.

At the back of the parking lot on the other side of the fence, I spot a mound of discarded scrap metal. Another second passes and the scrap metal moves with piercing screeches that ring out over the roar of the burning building behind me.

Black Magnet.

It's the first time I'm seeing him in the daylight. An assortment of metal pieces covers his body—car panels, corrugated roofing, Rachel's license plate—leaving a slit by his eyes to allow him to see.

There's definitely someone in there.

"Hey!" I bark and take off in a sprint toward him.

He takes off too, in the same direction that the wind carries the smoke from the burning building. The artificial darkness makes it seem like dusk, but still I hop the chain-linked fence and follow Black Magnet down Hickory Avenue along active industrial plants with several semi-trucks pulling in and out of parking lots, trying to navigate the narrow streets.

A truck turns in between us, breaking my view of Black Magnet completely. By the time it passes, I've lost sight of him. I run down a few blocks, trying to anticipate his direction of travel, but without knowing the city well enough, I can't anticipate where he might be heading.

Exhausted and gasping for clean air, I give up and decide to head back to ESTR.

Chapter Ten

"Thank God you're okay!" Rachel rushes to me when I get back to ESTR and wraps her arms around me. When she pulls away and notices my hand, she snatches it in hers. "You're hurt!"

"I'm fine." I try to tug it away, but she latches on.

"No, I need to take care of this." She pulls me over to the medic room and pats the edge of the hospital bed. "Sit."

She tugs off my gloves from the Heat suit and reveals my soot- and blood-covered hand. I'm definitely going to need a shower after she's done patching me up.

Perry comes in and leans against the doorframe. "So what exactly happened? You look like hell."

I wince as soon as Rachel pours alcohol on my wound. "Shit, that hurts!"

"Hold still!" She shifts her body to try to hide the equipment she pulled out of one of the drawers.

Perry gags and rushes to the trash bin.

"What's wrong with you?" I ask. "Dammit!" Another prick.

"Would you quit moving?" Rachel berates.

"I don't do blood," Perry mutters with his face inside the trash can.

"You're filthy!" she tells me. "What did you do?"

"I accidentally started a building on fire," I admit.

"You what?" Her head snaps up, scraping me with something sharp as she moves her hand.

"What the hell are you doing?" I bark.

"Well, if you would just *hold still*," she says. "Do I need to strap you down?"

As if this is my fault.

"Just let her do her thing, man," Perry's voice echoes from the plastic bin. "Just focus on me."

"Oh, because staring at your backside is so much better," I say.

He waves his hand toward me, still facing into the trash. "It's either my backside or my vomit. Your choice!"

I relent, so he asks, "How'd you manage to start a building on fire?"

"Yeah, the news said the chase was over," Rachel adds.

I squeeze my free hand into a fist and try to focus on something other than the pain. "It *was*—ah!"

"Almost done," she says.

"The driver took off and he led me to this old industrial plant of some sort," I explain. "When I got there, there were two other men and then all three of them started shooting at me."

Perry picks up his head. "A set up?"

"Maybe."

"So I'm assuming you missed when you were trading shots back and forth?" Rachel asks.

Perry catches a glimpse of my hand and dives back into the trash bin.

"I had excellent aim, thank you very much," I boast. "But

one of them ran into the building and I followed him."

"What was in there that caught fire?" She pulls away from me and says, "All done! And you didn't even cry."

I shoot her a look. "I don't know what was in the building, specifically. There was some kind of soot or something all over everything."

"Coal?" Perry chances another look at me.

"Maybe. I don't know."

"Coal mining used to be a major source of industry for Ellsworth." Rachel washes her hands at the sink.

"Oh." There's a piece of Ellsworth trivia I didn't know.

"Now one of the city's biggest industries is healthcare because a lot of the people who worked in the mines developed long term health effects," Perry adds. "Which warrants the need for ESTR and these lovely researchers in your presence."

"Well, at least something good came out of it," I say.

"Go back to the fire," Rachel says. "What happened?"

"The guy I chased in there was shooting at me and I tried to fire back—"

Perry rubs his forehead. "Oh, man, tell me you didn't do it."

"Well, we already know that I *did* do it," I murmur. "The whole place went up real fast, *but* I was able to get the guy I chased in there out safely."

"And did you stick around to make sure the fire department showed up?" Rachel goes to the next room and sits at her computer.

"Well, no because I saw Black Magnet." I follow her out with Perry on my tail.

"He was at the fire?" he asks.

"No, he showed up right after we escaped."

"Do you think he lured you there?" he asks.

I shrug. "That's what it seemed like to me. And it would've been nice to have some way of communicating back here so you guys could've told me *not* to light up an old coal plant!"

Perry scoffs. "Yeah, good luck with that. The device I was working on this morning failed a field test. *Miserably.*"

"You'll figure it out." Rachel points to her computer. "The plant fire is all over the news. Looks like they have it contained, but it's not out yet."

"There was a lot of coal in there," I say.

"Well yeah. The plant was open for almost a hundred years," Perry says. "Imagine how much was left over."

"I don't have to imagine it," I say. "I'm the one who lit it up!"

"Ash, you need to be more careful," she says. "Was anyone hurt?"

I shake my head. "Not that I know of. By the time I got that guy outside, the other two were gone and help was on the way."

"That's good at least." She gets up and heads back into the medic room to start cleaning up.

I stand in the doorway between the two rooms. "We need to figure out how Black Magnet fits into this. He ran off when I chased him."

Perry comes up behind me and I hand him the mask from my suit.

"Which reminds me," I say to him, "this stopped working when I ran after him. Not a lot, but I was definitely winded."

"The filter is probably clogged." He takes it from me and pops out the mechanism in the front. "How long were you in the smoke for?"

"Maybe five minutes, tops."

"Hmm, it should've been able to last longer than that," he says. "I'll have to make a few adjustments."

"Why don't you go home and get some rest?" Rachel suggests.

"First, I need a shower."

"Well yeah," she says. "And to change out of that Heat suit. We wouldn't want anyone arresting you for arson."

Great. How long is this going to be following me for?

Chapter Ten

"It's been a long day," I say.

"The day's not over yet."

"What do you mean?"

"Vernon's party's tonight."

Perry groans from his work table. "Crap, I forgot about that."

"And you both need to be well-dressed and ready to mingle," she says. "Especially you, Ash. You're going to be making first impressions tonight."

"Guess I better go downstairs and take a shower then." I limp from an ache in my leg that wasn't present before. Or, at least, not noticeable. Guess I took more of a beating than I realized. On the bright side, the ache in the opposite leg doesn't seem as noticeable.

Rachel's phone dings. "Vernon says he's on his way to take you home."

"Why?"

"I texted him and told him you had a rough morning," she says. "I'm sure he knew what I was talking about because every news station is covering it."

I curl my lip into a snarl.

"Let him take you home so you can get a nap in before dinner," she says. "Do you even have anything to wear tonight?"

"I don't know."

"I'm sure Vernon has something," she says. "If not, let us know and maybe Perry can help you out."

"I'm no one's personal shopper," he says from his work table.

She rolls her eyes and lowers her voice. "He'll make the exception for you."

"Thanks. I'm going to go scrub all of this soot off of me and try to forget the morning."

As I head downstairs, I wonder how much they worry about me. How much they talk about me when I'm not around. Do they see me as a threat? A flight risk? A basket case on the verge of a breakdown? Do they feel obligated to help me?

No. They're my friends. I'm just being paranoid. But what if it comes to a point where they no longer want to help me? Will they have the courage to tell me directly? Will I be okay with what they have to say?

The locker room in the basement is empty, as usual. I wonder if anyone actually uses it. Then again, it's the middle of a weekday. The people in this building are working now.

I strip off the Heat suit, stuff it in a locker, just in case, and examine myself in the mirror. Besides the soot covering my body, I've got bruises all over my legs, a bleeding hand—that's been stitched up thanks to Rachel—and several other cuts and scrapes along my arms. That's not counting the aches in my muscles and joints from the trip on top of the car. Or rather, the brutal landing.

The shower feels amazing, but it only helps to make me more tired. This morning took a lot out of me. By the time I get dressed—into a change of clothes I've learned to keep here at the lab—and make my way back upstairs, Rachel and Perry are already breaking for lunch.

She touches her lips as she finishes chewing her bite and then swallows. "Feeling better?"

I nod and lay my dirty Heat suit on one of the empty work tables. "Just tired. I'm going to take your advice and get that nap in."

"Good," she says. "You'll be well-rested for tonight."

"And you'll need it." Perry pops a potato chip into his mouth.

Rachel's phone dings again. "Perfect timing. Vernon's here. He's outside."

Perry points to the suit. "I'll get that all *buttoned up* for you, if you will."

I smile. "Thanks."

"Here, let me walk you out." He gets up and leads me down the hall.

Chapter Ten

When we're out of earshot of Lab #8, he asks, "Are you sure you're okay?"

I shrug. "Yeah. Just tired."

"I bet. Well, make sure you get some sleep before dinner."

"I will," I say. "See you guys later?"

"Wining and dining with Vernon and his pals isn't my idea of a fun night." He smiles. "But I'll be there for you. So will Rachel."

I turn toward the door, but he stops me.

"Just keep your eyes open," he says. "That chase and what happened at the building was clearly orchestrated for you. We need to figure out why. In the meantime, just be safe."

"I will. Thanks, Perry."

Chapter Eleven

"Look at that!" Vernon exclaims when I emerge from the bathroom in my room dressed to the nines in one of Vernon's old suits. "It fits perfectly!"

I step in front of the mirror and check myself over. I do look good. I wonder when the last time I was in a suit was, if ever.

"Thanks again for letting me borrow it for tonight." I reach for the tie and try to remember how to tie it. I'm not sure if I ever knew how.

"Oh, no problem." He notices me struggling and reaches for my neck piece. "Here, let me."

He loops it around his own neck and starts to tie it.

I take a seat on the edge of the bed. "To be honest, I'm really nervous about this dinner party."

"Nothing to be nervous about," he says. "Everyone will treat you with the utmost respect. I'll make sure of it."

I nod. "Yeah, I know. It's just...I don't know. Weird. I don't really fit in."

Chapter Eleven

He pulls the tie tight enough to hold its shape and then lifts it over his head and hands it to me. "You fit in because I say you fit in. You're *my* guest, as are the rest of the folks coming. Besides, I'm sure Rachel and Perry will be here soon."

I hook the tie around my neck and get it situated under my collar. Prom was probably the last time I wore a tie—pure speculation here. I'm not even positive how old I am. Was prom last year or five years ago? Did I even go?

"Who else is coming?" I tighten it up to my throat and pull down my collar.

Vernon steps closer and adjusts the back for me. "Just a few of my business associates."

"And they all think I'm a college student? What if they ask me about classes and stuff?"

He brushes lint off my shoulders and looks at me through the mirror. "Ash, you'll be fine." His phone buzzes. A moment later he says, "Hmm. I have to run into the office real quick."

Great. He's going to leave me here in a house full of people I don't know.

"Let's head downstairs. Everyone should be arriving anytime now. I'll need you to help entertain everyone until I get back."

He starts to the door and as we descend the stairs, I ask, "Do you mind if I come with you? I don't know anyone here."

"Don't worry. I'll be back before you know it."

Downstairs, Mia, the Michaels' main housekeeper, has already set the table. Through the open kitchen door, I spot Rosa working diligently at the stove.

The dining room is immaculately cleaned, not that it was ever really dirty or messy before. Now, the room looks like a showpiece straight out of a magazine. The long wooden dining table has been extended and covered with a black tablecloth that matches many of the fixtures in the room. There are several candles down the middle of the table with place settings already set at each seat. My apprehension only increases at the sight of it all.

Daniela steps through from the kitchen and approaches her husband. She looks just as perfect as she always does. "There you are. Some of our guests have just pulled up."

"Excellent," Vernon says with no trace of a smile. "I have to run into the office for a bit. Do you mind keeping them company with Ash until I return?"

She looks between us. "The office? But Vernon, most of our guests are your coworkers. They'll be here any minute."

"I know, dear, but this is for one of my clients."

She turns away from him, her lips pursed. "Very well."

He gives her a peck on the cheek and disappears through the kitchen.

The room is quiet as Daniela fusses with one of the flower arrangements. Orchids, draped onto the white tablecloth.

"Uh…your kids aren't going to be here?" It's my best attempt at making conversation.

She shakes her head. "No. They're not really ones for dinner parties. Besides, Peter has studying to do for his finals."

I nod and look around the room again in an effort to hide my envy. The nap I had earlier helped with the exhaustion from this morning's events, but it didn't help with my nerves about everything. Tonight being at the forefront of those nerves.

The doorbell rings and Daniela walks up to greet the first guests. I wait awkwardly in the middle of the open space with my hands in my pockets, trying to come up with something more natural I could be doing.

My shoulders relax when I see Perry step through the door. Although he's sporting his familiar thick-rimmed glasses, his dark curls have been smoothed back with hair product and he's traded his usual T-shirts for a suit similar to mine.

Behind him is Rachel. She's wearing a crimson cocktail dress and her blonde hair is braided into a bun on the top of her head. She's beautiful and I step forward with the intent to tell her so, but stop short when another man steps in behind her. Their hands are locked together.

Rachel's date has short-cropped dark hair and hard features. The navy blue suit he's wearing fits him just as it's designed to. When he steps through the door and the three of them walk over to me, he hooks his arm around Rachel possessively.

"We've come to save you, my friend," Perry says.

"Thanks," I say. Rachel might have a date, but at least Perry came alone. I can focus on him.

Great, I think. *How desperate am I thinking Perry could be my substitute date?*

"We figured we'd come early so you can have a buffer from all the new people," Rachel says. "You look great."

The smile comes easy. "Thanks. So do you."

Her date gives me a warning look, but she doesn't catch it.

"Oh! Ash, this is Evan. Evan, Ash."

He detaches his arm from her long enough to shake my hand before quickly retaking its place.

"Rachel never—" I stop myself from saying she never mentioned him. If I were in his shoes, that's definitely *not* something I'd want to hear.

"Where's Vernon?" she asks.

"He, uh, had to run out for a little bit," I tell her. "He said he wouldn't be gone long."

"Well, I see the drinks are being served," Perry says. "Ash, why don't we grab some for everyone?"

The two of us head over to the drinks table. With our backs turned toward Rachel and Evan, he mutters to me, "Don't make this more awkward than it is."

"What?"

"You know what." He offers a stern look and then glances at Rachel and Evan. "Let her personal life be her personal life."

I turn and look over at them. Rachel is smiling and pointing out different people. Evan nods, acknowledging who she's pointing to. He catches my gaze and I quickly turn back to Perry.

"Yeah, I will," I tell him. "No problem. I have bigger things to worry about anyway."

Like the fact that Rachel has her own personal life while mine only consists of Rachel and Perry. Other than Heat stuff, this is all I have in life. At least, that I remember. God, this is getting annoying.

"Don't forget that." Perry hands me a glass of champagne from the table near the kitchen and we head back toward Rachel and Evan. "Try to make an effort with him," he murmurs.

I nod, but don't offer anything else in case we're overheard. The crowd is thickening and the volume is increasing in the room.

"No drinks for us?" Rachel asks when we return.

"Oh shoot," Perry says. "I'm sorry. Here, let me go get you guys some."

"No, it's okay," she says. "I can get it."

Before either Evan or I can stop them, they both go back to the drinks table.

Make an effort. That's what I need to do.

I clear my throat. "So Evan, uh, where do you work?"

"I do design."

"Design? Like an artist?"

"Not quite."

"Oh, for advertising?"

"A little, yeah."

I smile awkwardly. "What's the other part?"

This is definitely harder than it seems.

"Computer stuff," he says. "Layout, typesetting, ad creation, that sort of stuff. You know, Photoshop."

I nod and take a sip, but the word doesn't resonate with me at all.

"What about you?" he asks.

"Me? Oh, I'm a, uh…student."

He raises an eyebrow. "Rachel said she worked with you at

the lab."

"She did? She did! I'm a, uh…I'm a…"

"You're a what?" Perry asks behind me.

I let out a deep breath. "Evan was asking me what I do at the lab."

"Oh! He's a, uh, he's a—" Rachel hands Evan his drink. "Well, he's doing a sort of internship with us."

"Right!" I exclaim. "An internship."

That makes sense. Too bad we're all such bad liars.

"So you're a biology major then? What year are you?"

"It's more of a, uh, general thing," I say. "You know, playing the field—the career field, that is."

"So, this is a great house, isn't it?" Perry interrupts. "Ash is lucky enough to be staying here while he's doing his…internship."

"Vernon must make a lot of money," I say.

"Well, it doesn't hurt that his father-in-law is a world-renowned surgeon," Rachel adds.

"Really?" I ask, genuinely curious.

"Oh yeah," Perry says. "I'm surprised Vernon hasn't pulled out the wedding photos for you. It usually only takes about ten minutes for anyone new he meets to see them."

Rachel points across the room to a portrait hanging above the fireplace. "They had that *painted* as a wedding gift to themselves."

I study it, finally making out the familiar shapes of a much younger Vernon and Daniela. I always assumed it was a painting of some long-forgotten couple, so I never gave it too much attention.

"All right, everyone." Vernon emerges from the kitchen and takes a glass of champagne from one of the servers. That really was a quick stop in to the office. "Take your seats. Dinner will be served shortly."

"Come on," Rachel says. "Let's make sure the four of us can

sit together. We'll go on the other side."

When she and Evan disappear around to the other side of the table, Perry and I find open seats on our side.

"Well, that was something," he says quietly to me.

"It was an effort," I reply.

"Call it what you want, it was still something."

Rachel and Evan arrive opposite us, but need to take an extra seat down. Rachel sits in the seat across from me and Evan sits to her left, across from the woman to my right. Perry sits next to me across from another stranger next to Rachel.

"Do you have enough room?" the woman to my right asks me. Her dark blonde hair is pulled up behind her in an intricate design of braids and clips, similar to the way Rachel's is. Except, you can tell Rachel did her own at home. I'm still partial to hers, though.

"Yup, I'm okay."

The woman extends her hand. "I'm Lisa, Vernon's assistant at River Valley."

I shake her hand and smile. "Nice to meet you. I'm Ash."

Recognition crosses her face. "Oh! You're the college student staying with them, right?"

I glance across to Rachel and then back to her. "That's me."

"Yeah, it's a shame that EIT didn't have any summer housing options open for you," she says. "Didn't they just open a new dorm building?"

"Uh…"

"It's full," Perry says from behind me. "Completely booked." He pats my shoulder hard. "This guy dragged his feet getting those forms filled out."

I smile because I don't have anything else to add. All I know of the Ellsworth Institute of Technology is the name and that I'm vaguely familiar with it.

"Oh, you should've been more attentive," she scolds with a smirk. "Now how do you know Vernon?"

Chapter Eleven

"Oh, um—"

"Lisa! You made it!" The woman across from Perry calls out. "You look great!"

Great. We'll spend all dinner stuck in between a conversation.

"Oh, thanks," Lisa says. "I was just talking to Ash. He's staying with Vernon and Daniela this summer."

The other woman reaches over and shakes my hand. "They're both great, aren't they? And this house!" She raises her hands and looks up.

I follow her gaze. "Yeah, it's nice."

Lisa motions to the woman and says, "This is Marge. She's one of the account managers."

"Crunching numbers, watching stocks, all that boring stuff," she adds. "How long are you staying with Vernon? Just this summer?"

"I, uh—I'm not sure." I look over to Rachel for help, but she's talking to Evan.

Perry comes to my rescue. "It's kind of on a wait-and-see basis." He reaches over to shake her hand. "I'm Perry Griswold. I'm one of the engineers at ESTR and a friend of Ash's."

"Oh, nice to meet you," Marge says. "I don't usually get to meet the people down in the trenches."

"Right, well, now you have."

The wait staff Vernon hired for the evening comes by and delivers each of us our salads, which diffuses a lot of the conversations. Thank God for that.

A small slab of meat serves as the main entrée. It's good, but not filling.

As I wait for the next plate to be set in front of me, I make small talk with Lisa. Rather, *she* talks about her time at EIT and I smile and nod along.

After dinner, everyone gets up and moves out to the patio on the side of the house, where the wait staff serves more drinks.

The four of us group together near the door, each with a drink in our hands.

"So how soon do you think we can acceptably sneak out of here?" Perry asks in a low voice.

Rachel shoots him a look. "We're here for Ash."

"No, it's okay," I say. "You guys can go if you want."

"All right, cool." Evan sets his drink on the nearest bar table and starts to turn to the door. Rachel grabs his arm.

"We're not going just yet."

"Ash!" Vernon calls from across the patio. "There's someone I'd like you to meet."

I give Rachel a look that says, "Help me," but there's nothing she can do. Setting my drink on the bar table next to Evan's, I walk over to Vernon, who is talking with his wife and an older man with a cane.

Vernon hooks his arm around my shoulders and motions to the man. "Ash, I'd like you to meet Arlus Cain, the owner of River Valley Holdings."

I reach for his hand, but when I look into his eyes I'm immediately struck with intense pain between my eyes. I manage to keep upright, but the discomfort is noticeable.

"Ash, are you okay?" Vernon's voice is distant, even though he's standing right next to me. "Get him a chair," he calls to someone.

In the next moment, I'm hit with another vision, similar to one I've already had. The boy I was beating up in my first vision is there. We're wrestling. No, fighting. Really fighting. Rolling around on a carpeted floor, trying to get the upper hand over the other.

Round and round we go, rolling on the floor, swinging punches at each other. Finally, the other boy grabs ahold of my throat and squeezes hard. Even though it's not real, I still feel myself suffocating. Rounding a firm punch into his gut, he loosens his grip and falls off.

Chapter Twelve

Reality sets back in and I feel strong hands ease me onto a chair by the door.

"Just relax," Vernon says. "Take it easy. It's okay."

"Ash, are you all right?" Rachel reaches for my hands.

I open my eyes and smile at her, but it's quickly wiped away when it hits me that all conversation has stopped. Everyone's looking at me. Vernon's beside me, a hand on my shoulder. Rachel's knelt in front of me. Perry and Evan are behind her.

"Maybe you should lie down," Mr. Cain suggests.

I scan the room again, unable to catch my breath. The added attention isn't helping, either. I'm not sure I need to lie down, but I do need to get out of here. From whatever triggered that vision.

"Yeah, I think that's probably a good idea," I say.

Perry pushes his way between Vernon and Rachel. "Here, I'll take him up. You can stay down here with your party," he tells Vernon.

"Are you sure?"

Leaning on him in an effort to prove that I need to go upstairs, Perry wraps his arm around me and leads me back inside. "Positive."

I don't get a chance to catch the look on Rachel's face before I'm conquering the stairs. Perry's help isn't required, but I keep up the act for whoever might be watching.

Once we're in my room, I shut the door and lock it behind us.

"We need to go," I say. "I don't want to stay here anymore."

I can't put my finger on it, but something no longer feels *right* at this house. The fact that I was never particularly comfortable here only adds to my decision.

Perry doesn't ask any questions. He finds my bag and starts stuffing the clothes Rachel bought me inside. "You better get out of that suit," he offers. "Just in case it's not an easy exit."

I grab some clothes and go into the bathroom to change into them. Gym shorts and a T-shirt. After being confined to formalwear for the last few hours, I've never felt more comfortable than I do right now.

What triggered that vision? They usually seem to have a trigger, but maybe that's not the case. Maybe it's just random. Maybe these visions don't mean anything.

No. They're too familiar. I *know* I was one of the boys I saw and I felt like I knew the other one. It's definitely pieces of my memory resurfacing. But why?

I need to talk it over with Rachel and Perry. But first, I need to get out of here.

"He's fine," Perry says from the other room. "I'm just going to take him back to my place so he can have some peace and quiet."

Who's he talking to? I go back into the bedroom to investigate.

"Just let me in," Vernon says from the other side. "I want to talk to him."

Chapter Twelve

I unlock the door and close it quickly behind him, relocking it. I feel safer with it locked and I don't know why.

"Are you sure you're all right?" he asks.

"I'm fine. Where's Rachel?"

"She and Evan went home."

Without checking to see if I was okay? Sure, Perry followed me up, but didn't she want to see for herself?

Vernon notices the bag Perry's struggling to zip up. It's filled to capacity. "That looks like a lot more than a change of overnight clothes."

"Yeah, he can stay with me." Perry manages to get the zipper closed. "This wasn't supposed to be a permanent arrangement anyway."

"But I have the extra room," he pleads. "Besides, how am I supposed to explain my guest of honor walking out in the middle of his own party?"

So this *was* for me.

"Is that really what you're worried about?" Perry asks. "Because I'm more concerned about making Ash comfortable and he says he wants to leave."

Vernon's eyes shoot to me. He looks hurt, but also worried.

"It's nothing personal—" The jiggle of the doorknob makes me jump and saves me from having to come up with an explanation.

"Hello? Vernon? Are you in there? Is that young man all right?" It's Mr. Cain.

Vernon turns to me with wide eyes. "Just a minute," he says loudly over his shoulder. Turning back to me, he drops his voice and says, "Grab your things and sneak out through the bathroom window. Follow the roofline to the back of the house and over the garage. There's a gate in the fence in the back. Stay away from the driveway and the side of the house. That's where the party is now. The back neighbors have a dog. He'll bark at you, but that's it."

"The bathroom?" I ask.

He puts a finger to his lips and again, shouts over his shoulder, "Ash isn't feeling well. I'll be out in a second." He says quietly to me, "Go. Quickly."

Perry pats Vernon's shoulder and nods before pushing me toward the bathroom.

"I hope it's nothing serious," the old man on the other side of the door says. "Should I call my personal doctor and have him come take a look at the boy?"

"No, I think he just needs a chance to rest." He waves at us to hurry.

Why the urgency? I was supposed to spend the evening with these people and now I need to sneak out? This can't just be for appearances.

Perry opens the bathroom window with a squeak and tosses the bag over onto the roof before climbing out himself.

"Why don't you go back downstairs?" Vernon calls to Mr. Cain. "I'll be down as soon as I'm done in here."

"What could you possibly be doing in there?" the man says.

The doorknob starts to turn and I dash into the bathroom, closing the door behind me.

"Where's the boy?" the man asks Vernon.

Hoisting myself up onto the windowsill, I stick my feet out first and slide—not as gracefully as I would've liked—out the window and join Perry on the roof.

"He's *really* not feeling well," Vernon says. "He's been in the bathroom since I got up here."

"I hope it's not food poisoning."

Their voices fade away as Perry and I move along the roof, sticking close to the outer wall of the upper floor. Perry has my bag slung over his shoulder. His dress shirt has come untucked and it hangs beneath his dress coat.

We climb down to the edge of the garage and Perry tosses my bag to the ground and jumps down after it. He looks around and gives me a thumbs up, so I follow suit, landing on the grass with a heavy thud. He snatches my bag and we race to the fence gate and through the neighbor's yard without tipping off the dog.

We make it to the street and turn left back to downtown, following Perry's lead. We don't stop running until we're a few blocks away.

Chapter Thirteen

Rachel's house sits on a street at the edge of town mostly devoid of any trees. It was a bit of a trek from Vernon's house, but we made it.

The first thing I notice when we approach is the mountain quite literally in her backyard. This is one of the most eastern streets in the city and it's right at the edge of the valley.

I follow Perry up the sidewalk pathway to the front door beside the single-car garage. The front of the ranch-style house is decorated with beautiful flowers of all different colors.

Perry adjusts my bag on his shoulder and knocks on the door. I've told him that I can carry it, but he still hasn't turned it over.

Through the glass door, I can see movement on the other side. A moment later, Evan answers. He's changed out of his navy blue suit and into a plain white T-shirt and black sweatpants. Looks like Evan's more than just Rachel's date for tonight.

"What's with the bag?" he asks.

Perry ignores his question. "Can we talk to Rachel?"

Chapter Thirteen

"Ash?" Rachel comes around Evan and wraps me in a hug. "You're okay!"

She pulls away and I notice Evan's scowl.

"Come in." She nudges Evan backward to allow us room to step inside. Straight back is the kitchen, the area to the left is set up as a living room, and behind that a small dining room table sits in front of a glass sliding door. There's a hallway off the living room that presumably leads to bedrooms.

Perry drops my bag on the floor.

"You moving in?" Evan asks.

That explains why Perry wouldn't let me take the bag. He must've known that Evan would be jealous.

"Sweetie, can you give us a minute?" Rachel asks him.

"No, it's okay," Perry says. "Why don't we just go outside to talk? Come on, Ash."

I follow him through the sliding doors and out onto the square concrete patio. The backyard is fenced in and nearby trees tower over us. The ones near the fence in the back hangs over the back half of the yard. Beyond that, the sharp incline up the side of the mountain starts.

We sit at a metal patio set just outside the door. The sun has set, but the air is still quite warm.

"He's my friend, Evan," Rachel yells inside.

"Then why did he bring a bag?"

"What am I supposed to tell him? No, you can't stay here because my boyfriend needs to claim ownership of me?"

"That's *not* what I mean," he counters.

Perry and I sit quietly. Any attempt at a conversation would be overpowered by the argument inside anyway. Instead, I study the paint chipping off the edge of the glass table. Anything to keep my eyes away from inside. If Evan knew we were watching them argue, that would only make things worse.

"I get what this looks like, but you need to trust me," she goes on.

He asks her something, but I can't make out exactly what. It's something about me, obviously.

"Go home," she declares. "Get your stuff and get out of here. I don't want to talk to you right now."

Several agonizing minutes later, the sliding door opens and Rachel joins us on the patio.

"Sorry about that," she mutters just before taking a seat.

"It's okay," Perry says quickly.

I offer a sad smile. "I'm sorry if I ruined your evening."

She sighs heavily. "It's only fitting to how it started. He was bitching about going to the dinner party and he was bitching as he walked out the door. I'm sorry we ditched you at the party earlier."

I shrug, trying to downplay my disappointment. "You probably just thought Perry had it handled."

"Well yeah, I did," she explains. "But I would've followed you guys up there if I didn't have Evan with me. After you left, he was badgering me to leave."

"Should I not have brought him here?" Perry asks.

She shakes her head. "No, I'm glad you did. I was expecting you to. That's another reason I agreed to leave. I figured Ash wouldn't want to stay at Vernon's with the party guests still there and I know your apartment doesn't have a lot of extra room and since I have an extra bedroom here..." She sucks in a deep breath and lets it go slowly. "Anyway, explain what exactly happened at the party."

"Well, I had another flashback...thing," I start.

Perry rolls his eyes. "We figured that much."

"What did you see this time?" Rachel asks.

"Well, that's the thing. It was basically the same vision that I had before."

"That's weird," Rachel says. "Which one?"

"The one where I was...wrestling with the other kid."

"Why do you think you experienced the same thing twice?"

Chapter Thirteen

she asks. "Do you think those scent tests are helping you remember?"

I shake my head. "It wasn't exactly the same. It was different, but the same kid was there."

"Weird." She leans back and furrows her brow in concentration.

"That's not the weird part," Perry says. "Think about what he was doing when he got the vision."

"He was meeting Arlus Cain," Rachel says. "So what?"

"So maybe he's somehow connected to Ash's life," he suggests. "Why else would he trigger a memory like that?"

"But if Mr. Cain knew him, why wouldn't he say something to him?" She holds up her hands. "I'm still going with scents here. Maybe he was wearing a cologne or something that reminded Ash of something from before."

I shake my head again. "I didn't really smell anything significant on him."

"Okay, let's figure some stuff out." Rachel pulls out her phone and sets it in front of her. "Oh, Vernon texted me."

"What did he say?" Perry asks.

"Just wants to make sure Ash is okay." She types out a quick reply and then says, "All right, so let's think."

"About what, exactly?" I ask

"Let start with the flashbacks," Perry says.

"Your brain is obviously trying to tell you something," Rachel adds. "We need to figure out what it is. What's the first flashback that you remember?"

I stare off into the neighbor's yard as I try to gather my thoughts. "Um…back when I first encountered the Gatekeeper."

She types it into her phone. "Okay, what did you see?"

I shrug. "It was just me wrestling with another boy."

"You as you now or you as a boy yourself?" Perry asks.

"I was a boy too," I respond. "Maybe like seven or eight—I don't know exactly."

Rachel types diligently into her phone.

"Any other important details?" he pushes.

I shake my head. "Not from that one, no."

"Okay, the next one?" Rachel asks.

"That was when we were at the mall."

"The mall?" Perry asks. There's a hint of annoyance to his words. "What happened at the mall?"

Rachel keeps her head down but doesn't say anything. I didn't tell her I had a vision there, but based off of my reaction at the food court, she probably guessed.

"Yeah. I saw a, uh, girl."

"A *girl*?" he asks. "Old girlfriend? Wait, *current* girlfriend?"

Rachel's typing falters for half a second.

I swat at Perry. "Shut up! I don't know."

She looks up from her phone. "How old was this girl?"

"She was a teenager, maybe. Early twenties at most."

"So your age?"

"Uh, yeah. I guess so." It's a strange feeling not knowing my own age.

"Any other important details about that flashback?"

I hesitate. There certainly were. That girl was special. Important. Evidently, not important enough to remember who she is. What if Perry is right and she *is* my current girlfriend? What other important people in my life have I forgotten?

"I felt like I knew her—I mean, I felt like I knew the boy in that first vision too, but she was…different. Like we were real close."

Perry smirks, but doesn't say anything else.

"Sister? Girlfriend? Best friend?" Rachel asks. "Do you remember a name?"

"Don't you think I'd mention if I remembered her name?" I snap.

"Okay then." She adds some more to her list.

"Sorry. It's just frustrating."

Chapter Thirteen

"Ash, we get it," Perry says. "We can only imagine how frustrating it is. But we're going to help you. In whatever way we can."

I offer a tight smile. "Thanks."

"So the next one?" Rachel asks.

"That was this morning, when I stepped inside that industrial plant."

"So it was the old coal plant?" she asks.

"I don't know."

"Maybe you have a connection to the coal mining industry," Perry suggests. "A lot of people in this city do."

"Yeah, but I don't think he'd have such a connection that it would remain in his subconscious," Rachel counters. "There'd be more important details of his life than that."

He shrugs. "It's an idea."

She nods and jots it down, then asks, "What did you see in that vision?"

I close my eyes to recall the memory. "I was running. There was smoke everywhere. Everything was dirty and dusty and smoky and…" I shake my head. "I think I was running into the cave."

"The one you woke up in?" Perry asks.

"Yeah, I think so."

Rachel taps her chin. "Interesting…"

I can tell all three of us are riding the same thought wavelength.

"Do you think that was when you got trapped in there?" she asks.

"I don't know," I say. "Maybe."

"What were you running toward?" Perry asks.

"I don't know," I say again. "All I saw were my footsteps hitting the ground. The smell, the dust. Just the feeling of being there, but not the reasoning."

Rachel chews on the inside of her cheek. "Hmm. That's weird."

"This whole thing is weird," Perry adds.

Her eyes grow as she studies her list. "That's for sure."

We're quiet as we all lose ourselves in theory. The cave I woke up in likely holds a lot of answers, but what if it holds just as many problems? What if Black Magnet is here to send me back to wherever I escaped from? But isn't that place here? Ellsworth feels familiar enough to me. I don't have any recollection of any other world. Of course, I don't have a recollection of really anything before I woke up in that cave. And what about the Gatekeeper? How does he fit into this?

"Well, we need to keep going." Rachel's voice breaks into my thoughts. "You had another one tonight."

I nod.

"Have you ever had two in one day before?" Perry asks.

I shake my head. "I don't think so."

"What did you see tonight?" Rachel asks.

"That same kid from the first vision—this time we were both a bit older, but I was beating on him."

"What do you mean?" she pushes.

"We were *really* fighting," I explain. "Nothing holding us back. We were swinging for the kill." My hand goes up to my neck at the memory.

"Both of you?" Perry asks.

"Yeah."

She types this all into her phone. "And that was when you met Arlus Cain?"

I nod. "I guess so."

"See!" Perry says.

"That's yet to be proven," Rachel says. "I still think something else triggered it."

"Either way, *something* triggered it," he says.

She turns back to me. "Is that it? Just those four flashbacks?"

I nod. "Yeah, I think so. But, I do have a funny feeling about this neighborhood."

Chapter Thirteen

"*My* neighborhood?" She's surprised, but smiles.

"Yeah. I don't think I've been here before, but it's like I've seen pictures of it or something…I don't know. It's hard to explain. It's familiar, that's for sure."

"Okay…" she says slowly. Confused.

"Do you think this is where you live?" Perry asks. "Do you recognize any of the houses?"

"Not specifically, no," I say. "It's just…familiar. I'm not sure how it all makes sense."

She sighs. "Well, people with amnesia are usually reminded of their past with familiar things that stir up repressed memories."

"Then what's the connection?" My frustration starts to rise. "Two of those flashbacks came when I came face-to-face with very bad people. Another one came when I was with you and, I'm sorry, but I don't remember you at all from before."

She sucks in her top lip and looks down.

"And the fourth vision came when I met Vernon's elderly boss," I finish.

"I wouldn't say Arlus is *elderly*—" Rachel says.

"His name is Arlus and he uses a cane," Perry says. "Yes, he's elderly. He's gotta be like seventy."

She breathes in a deep breath. "Okay, so what's your theory?"

He holds up his hands in surrender. "Hey, I'm still just gathering evidence. Ash, do *you* have any theories? You're the one living it."

I sigh. "I mean, Black Magnet didn't show up until I did, right?"

"Right."

I shrug. "So what if that means I brought him here? And the Gatekeeper. I'm the reason that old plant caught fire this morning, so maybe I'm also the reason for the raining infernos last week? What if even after I go away, Black Magnet stays and wreaks havoc because *I* brought him here?"

"Ash, you can't think that," Perry says.

"How can't I?" I counter. "None of this stuff happened before I woke up in the cave."

Rachel taps the table in front of me. "Hey, look at me. Even if you did bring them with you, I'm sure it wasn't intentional. Besides, that idea is garbage anyway. If you brought them with you, you would've seen them in the cave and you didn't, right?"

"I guess." My voice is small.

Perry shakes his head with a smirk. "You're not going to be rid of us that easily."

"And *you're* not going anywhere until we know for sure where you need to be, got it?" Rachel adds.

The sincerity and lightheartedness of their words breaks right through my depression.

"Thanks." I lean forward on my elbows and run my hands through my hair. "Ugh, my brain is so fried after the day I've had."

"Ordinarily, I'd laugh at a statement like that, but you *have* had a pretty rough day," he says.

Rachel and I both offer him looks.

"Oh come on! *Heat* is *fried*? That's gold!"

We both smile and roll our eyes.

Rachel locks her phone and holds it in her hand. "You know we'll find a solution to all of this, right? We'll get answers for you. It's just going to take some time."

"I know."

"Actually, I was thinking that maybe the cave you woke up in is a good place to start looking for those answers."

My head starts shaking before she even finishes. "No, Rachel. I get a bad feeling about that place."

"You don't have to go." Perry waves his hand between him and Rachel. "We can go and get samples or whatever and bring them back to the lab and—"

Chapter Thirteen

"No," I say firmly. "I don't want you guys going into that cave."

"We need some concrete evidence to go off of," she says. "Until then, we're just taking shots in the dark and that's not going to get us anywhere anytime soon."

"Yeah," Perry adds. "We'll take precautions. We'll be careful. I agree with Rachel that we'd be missing a real thread of evidence if we don't scope it out."

I let out a deep breath. I hate the idea of going back there—of letting my friends go in there—but what good would I be if I went with them? What if I have another flashback?

But they're right. It is a good place to start. Too many questions surround it. We need to scope it out.

"Okay, fine," I say. "We can talk about it later."

She smiles. "I'm glad you can be rational about this. And if you want, you can sit back at the lab and keep an eye—"

"No, I need to go with you."

Perry sighs. "Ash, you don't have to—"

"I need to show you guys where I woke up."

"Oh," he says.

"Yeah."

"I suppose that's true," she says. "Are you sure you'll be okay with that?"

I consider this. "I want answers. You're right. This is the only way to get them."

"Too bad we couldn't just ask someone," Perry muses.

"Like Arlus Cain?" I ask. "Why he was being so weird at Vernon's."

"Actually, yeah," he says. "That would make things a lot easier."

"Mmm, not if he actually has any malicious intentions," Rachel says. "And that's a big *if*."

"What do you know about him?" I ask.

"Not much, really," she admits.

"He's the owner of a lucrative company, so finding information on him shouldn't be too difficult with a Google search," Perry says.

"A what?" I ask.

"Google?" He hooks an eyebrow.

"You've never heard of Google?" she asks.

"Have you been living under a rock?" he adds.

I laugh. "Actually, yeah."

She points at me. "Okay, you got us there. Anyway, what made you guys rush out of Vernon's? I didn't expect you to show up for a few more hours."

"Just like Ash said, Arlus Cain was being weird," Perry says. "He *really* wanted to come in to Ash's room."

"Why?"

I shrug. "I don't know."

"What was with Vernon going to the office?" Perry asks. "Who would he be seeing on a Friday night? Especially when most of his coworkers were going to be at the party anyway."

"Do you think it had something to do with Arlus Cain?" Rachel asks.

"Maybe," I say. "But Vernon definitely didn't want me to leave because, you know, I'm the star of the show, apparently."

"I'm sure that wasn't the only reason." She holds up her phone. "He checked in to see how you were, didn't he?"

"True, but I was not getting good vibes from the whole thing," Perry says. "I mean, if someone—anyone or any*thing*—at that party triggered a vision for Ash, I wanted to get him out of there. I know we probably should've chased down the lead, but it left our boy vulnerable and that didn't sit well with me."

"No, getting him out of there was the right move." Rachel looks at me. "You're safe now. You can stay here tonight."

"I'll head home and see if I can brainstorm any ideas why Ash might've gotten a vision at the party." Perry turns to me. "You deserve a night off, especially after this morning."

Chapter Thirteen

This morning. Sheesh, that seems like it was so long ago.

"I'll call an Uber to take me home." He looks over to Rachel. "Do you mind picking me up to get my car in the morning? I don't really want to go back to Vernon's right now in case the party is still going on..."

"Sure, no problem," Rachel says.

As Perry taps away at his phone, I ask quietly, "What's an Uber?"

He rolls his eyes. "We really need to get your memory back."

"It's like a taxi," Rachel explains.

I nod. "Okay."

After another minute, he mutters, "The mountain isn't giving me good service here. You mind if I hop onto your Wi-Fi?"

She hooks a thump over her shoulder into the house. "Sure, the password's on the fridge."

After he's disappeared into the house, we're both quiet. All I can think about is the argument she and Evan had. The one that *I* caused just by being here. He shouldn't have flipped out like that. She deserves better. I'm not sure I can quite tell her *that*, but I can say something else.

"So...you have a boyfriend?"

She smiles and looks down. "Yeah, I do."

"I really am sorry for intruding."

She waves it off. "I don't mind. I even expected it, like I said. Evan's just...a hothead. He'll get over it. He doesn't get to tell me what to do."

"Good. I'd hate to see you let someone push you around."

"I don't let anyone push me around." She smiles again to try to convince me of that.

"Good," I repeat.

"Yeah."

I study the rusty tabletop as an awkward silence falls over us. After a few painfully slow moments, I clear my throat and bring up something that's been on my mind for a while.

"Hey, can I ask you a question?"

"Hmm?"

"Why did you take me in to ESTR? The day we met. After I fought off your attacker."

"You saved my life."

I look down at my lap. Anything to keep from meeting her eyes. "Well…"

"You were hurt," she says quietly.

"Yeah, but you could've just as easily called an ambulance."

"Ash, I saw you throw fire. I wasn't going to send you right to a hospital where God only knows what would've happened to you."

"Oh." I nod slowly and let out a breath of air. "Okay. So it was just a researcher's curiosity then?"

She must recognize my disappointment. "Well, yes. However, there was more to it than that."

My head snaps up to her. "There was?"

"Yeah. You were this mangy, gross looking man who ended up being my hero," she says. "You didn't know me and you just ran right up and helped me. I assumed you were homeless… until the flames appeared."

I chuckle. "That makes you even crazier for taking me in."

She shakes her head. "Nah. I could tell that underneath all that grime was a good person with a big heart and I couldn't just send you off to someone else. I wanted to make sure you were okay. I *still* want to make sure you're okay."

I look up and smile at her, but she's staring at her lap, fidgeting with her fingernails.

"I guess you saved my life that day too," I tell her. "Thank you."

She looks up and returns my smile. "I'd do it again in a heartbeat."

Chapter Fourteen

"You hungry?" Rachel asks me the next morning after I've emerged from the hall bathroom. She's in a white tank top and green shorts.

"What do you have?" I'm wearing the T-shirt I had on under my suit last night and a pair of gym shorts. I shuffle over and sit at the breakfast bar.

"Cereal." She opens a cupboard and pulls out a box of Cheerios. "I think I might have some fruit in the fridge if you want to add that."

I shake my head. "This will be fine. I could use some coffee, though. It was a long night."

"Sure thing." She pulls a mug out of a different cupboard and turns toward the coffee pot. "How'd you sleep?"

"I slept okay. The bed was comfortable, but…"

"Not your bed?"

"No." More than that, I could've done without waking up every half an hour in a panic, worrying that I was trapped in the cave again. I should've asked her for a night light or something. The complete darkness didn't help.

The coffee begins trickling into the cup.

"Wow, that's fast."

"It's nice, isn't it?" she says with a smile. "Not like in college when we had to make a full pot. Thank God for Keurig."

"For what?"

"Never mind. Oh! A bowl would help." Opening a third cupboard, she pulls out a bowl and digs through a drawer for a spoon.

"Aren't you having anything?" I pour the contents of the yellow box into the bowl.

She shakes her head. "I'm not really hungry. I know it's not the most healthy start to the day, but..."

"Last night still on your mind?"

"Uh-huh." The coffee finishes pouring and she carries it over to me. "But we have plenty of time to worry about that later today. Let's just enjoy the morning."

I look through the sliding door out onto the patio. The sun shines brightly through the windows, lighting up the whole house.

"It's a beautiful view." I motion with my spoon.

She turns and looks back. "Yeah, I love it. Too bad some days I'm up so early I can't really enjoy it."

"How long have you lived here?"

"Just about two years," she says. "Once I realized that my job at ESTR was permanent."

"Didn't River Valley commit to the funding?" I raise the bowl and drink up the milk.

"Yeah, but I've started jobs before with that same promise. Six months later I'd be in the unemployment line."

"How many places did you work before the lab?"

Chewing her bottom lip, she counts off on her fingers. "Well, let's see: before the lab, I worked on a project for EMG and EIT."

Chapter Fourteen

"Where you met Perry."

"Right. Oh, well right after I finished med school, I thought I might want to work with patients, so I got a job at the First Olympian Medical Center. I realized I hated that and moved to a private practice, also in Olympia." She shakes her head. "That whole office was mismanaged when it came to finances so that soon closed. That's when I started doing research for Wilkinson College in Olympia, but—surprise surprise—they weren't as committed to funding as I wanted them to be. But EIT noticed me and offered me a lot more money than what I had ever made."

"What happened with that?"

"They kept stringing me along, telling me they were waiting for this or that to fully commit to my funding for a long-term permanent position. Eventually, they admitted that it probably wasn't coming and laid me off."

"Ouch."

"Yeah. Especially after I had moved here from Olympia. It's not like they're that close."

"Not at all." That much I remember.

"After about a month of being an unemployed college grad, I got a call from EIT saying they were approached by EMG to develop 'advanced technological breakthroughs in modern sciences.'"

"Huh?"

"Medical technology, basically," she clarifies. "That was the job where I met Perry and we worked on ways to better perfect cancer-detecting software."

"How did that go?"

"Pretty well," she says. "It's what spring boarded our jobs at ESTR, but it wasn't a full time gig."

"So when you heard about ESTR, it was a no-brainer."

"Exactly."

"Well, I'm glad you landed on your feet."

She sighs and looks out the front window. "Yeah, I guess."

"You don't like your job, do you?"

"No, I love it," she says quickly. "I just wish I could better rely on the funding. I'm always afraid that I'm going to lose my job, but I guess that's what working in research is."

"Hopefully this thing with River Valley is permanent."

"Yeah." She looks down at her phone. "Shoot, we need to get going. Do you mind if I hop in the shower first?"

"Go right ahead, it's your house."

"Thanks, Ash."

"Well, thank you for letting me stay last night."

She offers a smile and disappears into her room.

"SO I'VE BEEN thinking," Perry later that morning at ESTR. "I don't think we're quite ready to explore the cave just yet."

"Why's that?" Rachel sets her bag onto her desk and cradles her coffee in between both hands. She brought it from home in her fancy coffee pot.

"Well, we don't really know what we're looking for and we don't really even know what's in there," he says

"He's got a point," I say.

Rachel shoots me a look. On the car ride in, I tried to talk her out of going to the cave. It didn't work.

"Okay." She plops down at her computer and types away at the keyboard. A moment later, the screen lights up. "I actually have a hunch that I want to look into real quick."

"What's that?" Perry asks.

"Just give me a minute." She types more on the keyboard and clicks around with the mouse.

"How'd last night go?" Perry asks me quietly.

I shrug. "It was fine. Kind of weird, but I'm glad I wasn't at Vernon's."

"If you don't mind crashing on the couch, we can get you

set up at my place tonight," he says. "I think that'd be best for everyone."

I nod, understanding that he means it'd be best for Rachel's relationship with Evan.

"I knew it!" she exclaims from her desk.

"Knew what?" Perry asks and we both venture over to her computer.

"That building that Ash started on fire *was* the old coal mining plant!"

"Okay," he says. "We kind of already figured that. It explains the combustibles."

"I can vouch for that," I add.

"Right, but according to this article I found by the city historian, the coal was mined from tunnels dug into the rock, brought to the plant by a conveyor belt down the side of the mountain, and cleaned and packaged at the plant."

"But the plant was in the middle of the city," I say.

She shakes her head. "Not when it was at full capacity." She scrolls down the page with her mouse. "Here's a picture of what it looked like in its heyday."

I lean in closer and take a look at the black and white aerial shot of the plant. It's nothing like it was yesterday. The picture shows several buildings—warehouses, mostly—shoehorned into a tight street grid. From what I can tell, most of those warehouses have been torn down for vacant parking lots.

"Most of the buildings have been condemned and demolished over the years." She points to the screen to indicate what buildings she's talking about. "See how they butt up against the mountain here? All of that is blocked off now. The conveyor belt would've run down the side straight into one of the warehouses."

"Yeah, I think you could technically follow the path up there," Perry adds.

Just like the one I took on the way down the mountain after I woke up in the cave.

"Okay, so you think the cave was actually the entrance to the coal mine?" I ask.

"That's *exactly* what I think," she says with a grin. "The cave obviously smelled like coal, so when you went into the plant and smelled coal, you had that flashback. *That's* the trigger."

Perry shrugs. "It makes sense."

"Of course it does," she says. "Remember what he looked like when he first showed up?"

"Covered in soot?" Perry says.

She nods and looks at me. "And I'm willing to bet that all of your other visions were triggered by some other connection to your past. Ash, if we can piece together this puzzle and keep triggering your memory, we'll be able to figure out who you are."

"That's all fine and nice, but I don't see how the Gatekeeper, the mall, and Arlus Cain relate to me specifically," I say. "They each triggered a vision for some reason."

"That's what we have to figure out," she says. "But I really do think the cave is the best place to start."

Even I can't argue with that, but still, the thought of going back there makes me squirm. Something bad happened there—maybe even before I arrived. All my warning signs go up at the thought of reentering it with my friends.

Apparently, Perry notices how uncomfortable I am.

"Not today," he says. "First, I think we need to spend a good amount of time researching the cave."

"What did you have in mind?" Rachel asks.

"Well, we have no idea what's up there—what's been publicly documented since the coal mines closed or what's *really* in there. We'd be going in blind if we went in now."

I nod. "That's true."

"All right, I guess I can't argue with that logic."

"So let's spend the week doing some research and then we'll head up there next Saturday," he says.

"You want to wait another week!?" she blurts.

Chapter Fourteen

He shoots her a look. "Rachel, you're a researcher. You know we can't collect all of the data in one day." He waves his arm over at me. "Besides, look how nervous Ash is about going back in there."

I try to act casual, but it's no use. I'm too tense from being called out. Doesn't help that the whole conversation revolves around me anyway.

Rachel tries to meet my eyes, but I look away.

"Okay," she finally says. "We'll take more time to gather data. I'll stay here and look into what was left in the cave after the mines closed, what they've done to it since, and try to get a reading of any toxic chemicals still present at the site other than the obvious. Oh, and I'll be determining the flammability radius too. Just in case."

Perry snaps his fingers and points at her. "Fantastic! In the meantime, I'll try to get our boy into shape!"

That catches me off guard. "Wait, what?"

"Ash, if you're going to be Heat, you need to live up to a certain standard," he says. "Physically and...pyrokinetically."

I narrow my eyes. "What?"

"Your abilities," Rachel translates.

"Yeah." He snaps his fingers. "Get your suit. We can go now and give Rachel some quiet time to work."

She rolls her eyes. "Oh, how generous. You sure this has nothing to do with you looking for an excuse to get out of work?"

He feigns surprise. "I would not! This is simply my way of helping out a friend."

We laugh.

"What he's saying makes sense, though," she tells me. "You need to make sure you're the best you can be if you're going to go after criminals—not to mention people like Black Magnet or the Gatekeeper. Police go through training, too."

I sigh. "Yeah, you're right."

Perry raises his hand, as if he's a student waiting to answer a question. "I think we need to make something clear, though. It's probably in our best interest if we limit how much we tell Vernon. Namely, us eventually going to the cave."

"You don't trust him?" I blurt.

Perry looks up and opens his mouth to say something, but closes it again as he considers the best way to go on. "It's not that I don't trust him. I mean, we've been friends with him for years. But since Arlus Cain was acting so weird last night at Vernon's dinner party—"

"And Mr. Cain potentially also triggered one of your flashbacks," Rachel interjects.

"Good point," Perry says. "That's even more reason to keep this to ourselves. Somehow Arlus Cain is connected to your past and Vernon knows him personally as well as professionally. While I don't think Vernon would intentionally rat you out, it's probably better if he stays in the dark about the details in case something might come up in conversation."

"I agree," Rachel says. "Let's hold our cards close. We don't really know what we're up against. Can't be too careful."

MY BODY IS consumed in flames. I whiz through the air, chasing each of the tennis balls the launcher shoots in my direction. Even though I reach for each of them, they burn to ash before I can get a firm grasp on them.

It has to be around a hundred degrees out and we're in an open field where there's no shade cover. Even if my body can take the heat from my abilities, the sun is still brutal.

Perry waves me down from beneath the pop-up tent at the back of the van. As I land next to him, the flames extinguish. I step under the shade where he has a lounge chair and a few pieces of tech. I still have no idea what they all do.

"Geez, dude." He wipes the sweat from his brow with his T-shirt sleeve and then replaces his eyeglasses, followed by a pair of sunglasses. "As if it wasn't hot enough out here already, you had to turn into a bonfire right next to me."

I smile and pull off the mask so I can wipe away the sweat from my own brow. "Sorry. I did good, though, huh?"

We've been out here all day, working on endurance, speed, temperature, everything Perry could think of. We've been training all week. Since we've already done a couple training sessions—not to mention the first-hand experience I've had—I pretty much have the hang of my powers by now.

He pokes around at his tablet. "You did excellent. You hit more than ninety percent of the targets, your record high speed was sixty-three miles per hour, and your average was forty-two."

"Plus, I'm managing the full body flames better than I was."

"Very true." He closes up the case on the tablet and sets it in the back of the van. "I don't know about you, but I'm tired of this heat—no offense."

I chuckle. "Was that intentional?"

"Actually no, but I guess my wit just comes naturally." He fires a finger gun at me with a click in the corner of his mouth. "Come on. Help me load everything up and then we can head back to the lab so Rachel can input today's data."

Perry grabs some of the pieces of tech and starts loading them back into the various bags he brought them in, piling them carefully in the back of the van.

"Yeah, just give me a minute to change out of this suit." I go around to the passenger seat and grab my bag, leaning back onto the seat as I pull off my boots so I can start to peel the leather suit off of me. "I'm sweating like a pig in this thing."

"Yeah, I know," he says from back by the tent. "I'm still working on that comm piece Rachel wants you to have, not to mention my *actual* job. You're lucky you have a suit at all."

I fall back onto the seat as I yank at the suit to get it off my legs. I'm more tired from this than the practice all day. "Well, thank you for—*ergh!*—coming up with that much."

"I did manage to fix your mask, though," he says. "Put it a whole new filtration system, so it should hold up to even the smokiest of places."

"Let's hope I'm never in a situation like that." Finally, I manage to pull the suit off and toss it on the floor of the van.

"Yeah. Are you done yet?" he asks. "I need your help taking down this tent."

"Give me a minute." I pull on a pair of gym shorts and wipe the sweat off my brow with the bottom of my T-shirt, but it's soaked. Instead, I pull it off and toss it next to the Heat suit.

He raises his eyebrows when he sees me come around the corner of the van. "I hope you're not doing that to impress Rachel, because she's taken."

"I know and it's not." I fight the urge to roll my eyes. "You ready to go with this tent?"

He goes to the opposite corner and we both grab an end and walk it to the middle until it folds up.

"So nothing happened last night?"

I narrow my eyes. "You think I'd put the moves on her mere hours after discovering she has a boyfriend?"

He hooks an eyebrow. "'Put the moves on'? No, Ash, I didn't think you turned into Sammy Smooth or something, I just meant—I don't know—was it awkward or anything? What did you guys talk about? That sort of thing."

I help him lift the tent into the back of the van and then the table and chair.

"No. She gave me some extra blankets, pointed out the bathroom, and then we went to bed—separately." I was too tired to even think of staying up and chatting.

"What about this morning?" He closes the back doors and moves up to the driver's seat.

I open the opposite door and pull on a dry T-shirt before hopping in and pulling on my seatbelt.

Chapter Fourteen

"She made me coffee, I took a shower, and then we picked you up to get your car from Vernon's," I say. "Nothing happened."

The air conditioning finally starts to cool the air as Perry drives slow over the bumpy field back to the road that leads into the city.

"That's good," he says. "Tonight I'll have you crash at my place. Actually, that might be the best long-term solution for now. I hope you don't mind sleeping on the couch."

"No, that's fine. I'll be getting up at the same time as you anyway."

"True. Tomorrow, you and I are starting bright and early. No excuses. You did great today, but now it's about stamina. How long you can keep this firepower stuff up, you know?" He pulls onto the road and the engine roars as it gets to speed.

"Okay."

"I'm sure Evan will be relieved that you're no longer her houseguest," he says.

"It was one night."

"An *unplanned* night," he clarifies.

"What's his deal anyway?" I ask bravely. "He seemed to be…"

"Kind of a grouch?" He shrugs. "I mean, if a random guy showed up and asked to spend the night at *your* girlfriend's house, wouldn't you be a little jealous?"

I think of that girl from my vision. "Yeah, I guess."

"They haven't been together long," he goes on. "He's all right. He's not bad. I've only met him a couple times. We haven't really chatted. He's not…my type of person, you know?"

"What do you mean?"

He laughs. "I mean, I'm a nerd. He's a little bit more macho."

"Oh."

"Don't get involved!" He wags a finger at me.

"I know," I say.

"For all you know, you could be married or something. When you finally remember, that's going to be a messed up situation if you don't keep your distance."

I wish I knew a name or had a tangible picture of that girl from my vision to show around and—

And what? Flash her picture around town like *she's* the one who's missing? Just another way that I'm stuck with my circumstances.

We make it back to ESTR and I get a few strange looks as we walk back to Lab #8. I've already soaked through this T-shirt. I probably stink, too. Maybe I'll have to use the basement shower again.

In the lab, Rachel's packing up her things for the day.

"Oh, you guys are back," she says with surprise. "I figured you'd just head home from wherever you were."

"Hold on! Don't go anywhere!" Perry tells her as he marches to his computer and plugs something into it. "I want to download the data we got today so you can take a look at it."

"It was a good day," I tell her. "We went out to some field outside of the city."

She nods. "Well, at least it was time well spent. I got a lot of things done myself. But I'm glad you guys are here."

"Why?" I ask. "Did something happen?"

"Well…sort of. Vernon stopped by while you were out."

Perry looks up from his computer. "What did he want?"

She shakes her head. "Nothing really. Just said that he wanted to check out his investment—"

"Nothing about Ash?" Perry blurts.

"Not until on his way out," she says. "I mean, he texted me last night, so he already knew you were fine."

"Didn't he wonder where we were?" I ask. "Or wonder if I was staying at his place tonight?"

She shakes her head. "He didn't say."

Perry exchanges glances with me and then turns back to Rachel. "That's weird."

"Yeah, and he didn't really seem like himself," she adds.

Chapter Fourteen

"How so?" I ask.

"Just kind of awkward," she says. "Nervous, fidgety. Very jumpy. I even felt kind of uncomfortable."

"What's going on with him?" Perry asks.

"I don't know, but it's a good thing Ash isn't staying with him anymore."

"No, he'll be safe at my place tonight," he says. "First thing in the morning, we'll be out practicing his powers some more."

"Good," Rachel says. "I think we should be prepared for anything."

Chapter Fifteen

After pulling the phone cord tight around the female burglar's wrists—Tina Platton, according to what Perry dug up before I left—I stand up and turn to the bank manager. Patty, as it says on her name tag. She's crouched in the corner of the bank vault, staring at me with wide eyes. Despite a few of my pictures being on the news from last week's high-speed chase, most people probably haven't seen me as Heat. The red leather and flaming hands should certainly be memorable, though.

I'm at the Ellsworth National Bank downtown, responding to one of Perry's alerts about a bank robbery. A hostage situation, actually. Luckily, I managed to sneak in the back, which is where I discovered Miss Platton cleaning out the vault with a gun pointed at Patty.

"Are you're all right?" I offer my hand to help the bank manager up, but she doesn't take it.

"Y-Yeah." She rises to her feet on her own and brushes lint

Chapter Fifteen

off her black skirt, trying to regain her composure. "There's a man up front. He has a gun. I've already called the police."

I glance back out down the hallway. Perry told me there was a man in the lobby and I should've expected him to be armed. Rookie mistake. At least I'm packing heat too.

"Okay." I turn back to Patty and point to Tina tied up on the floor. I managed to sneak up on her and knock her out, so she's not moving. "I need you to watch her while I go take care of the front."

"But—the police—"

I shake my head. "The police aren't going to enter the building until they're sure that they can get everyone out safely. I need to make sure that she doesn't get away either. Can you do that?"

She doesn't look confident, but nods anyway. With no other options, I exit the vault and race down the hallway toward the lobby.

Keeping low, I move to behind one of the cubicle spaces separating the hallway and the rest of the lobby. Peering around the corner, I see a group of bank employees and customers seated in the middle of the open room. Most of them are adults, but I do spot a teenaged girl huddled with her mother.

Silently, the gunman—James Malloy—walks slowly in front of them, his rifle propped up on his shoulder. The slow steps of his boots are like a timer ticking away on a bomb.

How the hell am I going to get the hostages out of here safely without Malloy shooting one of them in the process?

I wait until he's at the other end of the group with his back turned to me, but one of the hostages notices me. Then another. And another. Soon most of them stare in my direction, hoping I'm going to help them.

Malloy turns and points his gun at me. I dive back behind the cubicle to get out of his sight. Bullets tear through the faux walls as I army crawl to the other end.

"So you're the mysterious man in red," he says once the bullets stop flying.

Confident that he won't hit me, I rise to a crouch and close the distance to the end of the cubicle, which butts up to the counter the tellers stand behind.

Rising to my feet and breaking into a sprint, I launch myself over the counter, swinging my arm and releasing a stream of flame out toward the window by the sidewalk outside. Shifting my focus quickly has been part of my training with Perry all week.

There are several screams from the group and most of the hostages duck down and cover their heads. Even the shooter seems to be momentarily stunned.

Police cars pull up with squealing tires on the pavement. The car doors swing open and the officers get behind them for protection with their weapons raised toward the building.

"Go!" I shout at the hostages.

Several of them run out as soon as I tell them to, others hesitate for a moment before realizing it's their best opportunity for escape.

Malloy points his gun at them and I raise my hand to throw fire at him again, but instead he reaches out with his free hand and grasps the teenaged girl as she tries to flee. Her dark hair falls in her terror-stricken face and she yelps when he grabs her, stifling a whimper. Her thin-strapped purse falls to the ground beside her, spilling out her phone, keys, and a can of hair spray that rolls all the way to the door.

"Don't you touch her!" her mother shouts at him near the broken window.

He pulls the girl next to him and points the gun at her. "Which one of you should I shoot then? You or her?"

The woman glances at me quickly and then returns her eyes to Malloy and her daughter.

"Hey!" I shout at him to get his attention. "Easy." I hold out my hands as a warning. "I don't want anyone to get hurt."

"You're the one who started throwing fire," he snarls. "Where's Tina?"

"She's already in police custody." That's not exactly true, but it's close enough.

"Just let me go then," he says. "Or I'm shooting someone."

The girl whimpers some more.

"Just look at me, baby," her mother says. "Right here at me."

"Okay, okay," I say to bring Malloy's attention back to me. "The police are right out front, so let's go to the back."

He pulls the gun away from the girl's head long enough to wave me toward the hallway. "You first, Red."

"Let the girl go." I can't attack if he still has his gun pointed at her.

"You'd rather me shoot you?"

I swallow hard. "Yes."

Not wasting any time, he points the gun at me and just before he fires, I throw both of my hands in front of me and create a wave of flame. Dropping to the floor, I duck down out of range of the gun. Seconds later, one lone bullet flies through the fire and lodges into the wall behind where I was standing.

When the flames subside, the girl is lying on the floor and her mother is rushing toward her.

"Oh, baby, you're okay!"

They're clutching to each other, both sobbing.

The mother looks up for a moment and points down the hall. "That way!"

"Thanks." I sprint to catch up to Malloy.

He makes it halfway down the hallway before I'm on his tail. He throws his arm back and shoots at nothing in particular as he sprints to the emergency exit.

Ducking to one side to dodge the bullets stalls me enough so that he nearly reaches the door. Bursting into flames, I hover above the floor and shoot down the hall. We collide and I wrap my flaming arms around him. They disperse as we fall to the floor.

Malloy struggles to get away as his clothes continue to burn, but I have him pinned face-down beneath me.

"Careful, or the next thing I light on fire will be you." I slam my fist against his wrist and he releases the gun. I push it away and hold his arms behind him.

Lifting him to his feet, I lead him to the front lobby and out the doors. Police rush to me and take Malloy from my grasp. Within a matter of minutes, there are handcuffs slapped on his wrists and he's in the back of a police car.

One of the officers approaches me. "Do you have a minute?"

I debate whether it's a good idea to talk to him, but then if I don't and leave the scene, the police might think that I have reason to be guilty. They might even try to connect me with the firestorm from last week.

"How can I help, officer?" I eye up the quickest way to escape if I need to. The place is mobbed now with first responders, hostages, and other witnesses. The best bet would be to go up if I need to.

"What's your name?"

"Heat."

His eyebrows go up. "Heat?"

"Yes."

"I mean your real name—and can we lose the mask?"

I shake my head. "I'd rather not, sir."

"Why not?"

I point to the police car. "James Malloy was working with a woman named Tina Platton. She's tied up in the vault with the bank manager standing guard. Oh, and check to see if her bag is full of money. I didn't get a chance to. You know, mad man with a gun in the lobby and all."

The officer relays the information through his walkie-talkie on his shoulder.

Chapter Fifteen

"We'll get someone on it. What were you doing inside?" He indicates my suit. "I'm guessing you weren't making a deposit."

I smirk, but he doesn't see it under the mask. "No, sir. I was just doing my civic duty."

Civic duty? Who the hell says that?

"Uh-huh," he says disbelievingly.

"Look, I know it probably doesn't mean much, but I just want to help people," I tell him. "No ill-intentions at all."

The man nods. "Okay."

"Now, if you'll excuse me, I think I'm all done here."

"Actually—"

I don't hear the rest of his sentence as I burst into flame and shoot up into the air.

Stopping a burglary and saving a bunch of hostages? Not a bad way to start the day, that's for sure.

"WELCOME BACK, MR. HERO!" Perry offers a high-five when I come through the door, sweaty and smiling. He's standing next to his desk in a black sweatshirt. A little odd for the summer, but the air conditioning in here can be a little chilly.

"It was pretty awesome," I admit. "Thanks for training with me all week. It really paid off."

"No problem. I'm glad it helped."

"It really did." I set my bag on one of the work tables.

Perry showed me the roof entry this week so I've been using that when I go out as Heat. That way I'm not spotted by anyone else in the building. It's a risk that I don't like taking, but it's better than walking through the halls in my suit. And it allows me the privacy to change out of the suit on the roof. The extra precaution isn't needed today because it's the weekend, but it's still a good habit.

"But you have to keep at it," he says. "Use it or lose it."

"Yeah! You ready to go train some more?"

Perry turns to Rachel.

"Uh, we have something to do today," she says from her desk.

We both turn to her.

"You forgot, didn't you?" she asks.

I stare blankly.

"It's Saturday," she says. "We're going to check out that cave."

Right. I've been dreading this all week and in the excitement of this morning, I had forgotten about it.

"I've done as much research into it this week as I could," she says. "The mines closed in the late sixties after a fire killed fifteen of the workers."

"I remember hearing something about that from my parents growing up," Perry adds. "I didn't realize that's why it closed."

"Well, that and there were other methods of collecting coal that weren't so dangerous," she says. "Plus, nowadays there's a push toward greener energy sources. I mean, look at what Olympia's doing with all of the solar energy."

"It's nicknamed the Solar City," Perry says.

"Yeah. Anyway, when the mine closed, the plant did as well. The property—which included the cave—went into foreclosure and the city took possession of it. But other than blocking off the path to the cave—"

"Which is just a chain-link fence," I add.

"Then I guess they haven't really done anything to it," she says.

"It's just sitting there?" Perry asks.

She nods.

"Any radioactivity?" he asks. "What were the toxicity levels?"

"All within the normal ranges," she says. "Guys, for all intents and purposes, this place is safe."

"Well, I mean, you don't know the structural integrity of the cave," Perry says. "Or the harmful chemicals that could've contaminated the air."

Chapter Fifteen

"True, but it's not like we're doing much digging," she says. "We're just walking. We'll wear masks and be careful if we decide to take samples."

"Okay," I say with a sigh. "Let's go, then."

"We've already loaded up the van," she says.

"Yup," Perry says. "Masks, oxygen, lights, helmets, the whole shebang is in the van already."

She nods and continues, "Judging from maps I found online and what you've told us from what you remember, we know that there's a path up there—"

"Up where?" Vernon asks, stepping into the lab.

Chapter Sixteen

I'm surprised to see him at first until I remember that it's the weekend. Vernon doesn't have to work. Neither should Rachel and Perry, actually. But then, they're sacrificing their time off to help me.

The three of us exchange looks.

"To the cave I woke up in," I finally say. "Rachel thinks we should check it out because it might hold some clues that would explain what happened to me. How I ended up there."

"Are you sure it's safe?" he asks.

"As sure as we can be," she says. "I've been looking into it all week. From what I can tell from here, there aren't any significant harmful chemicals, no sign of deterioration, and the possibility of wildlife in there is minimal. I've done all I can, short of actually going there."

"It's still pretty risky, but I guess we've decided that it's worth it," Perry adds.

"Okay," he says. "I'll tag along. You can always use an extra—"

Chapter Sixteen

"No," Perry blurts.

Rachel shoots him a look and then turns to Vernon. "He just means that we don't want to put anyone else in danger if it turns out I missed something."

Vernon waves it off. "You're good at what you do. I'm sure you've scoped it out better than any of us could—minus Perry, maybe."

"Okay, Vernon, you can come if you want," I say. "Let's just all be careful."

We're all quiet as we close up the lab. I escape to the bathroom to change into my Heat suit before we all head out to the van in the back parking lot. Perry gets behind the wheel and pulls out of the lot toward the mountainside.

My heart beats faster and my skin feels clammy, despite the air conditioned vehicle. When Perry pulls up to the fence, he gets out with a bolt cutter for the chains blocking our path up the mountain. Once he's back in the van, I watch nervously as he navigates the narrow path up to the cave.

"Be careful." Rachel holds on to the front seat and stretches to look out the windshield in front.

In the passenger seat, I stare at the city stretched out beneath us as we rise higher and higher up the mountain. I try my best to forget our destination.

It doesn't help.

The closer we get, the more my anxiety builds. My back is soaked with sweat, not from the heat or my suit, but from nerves. My fingers are ice cold and my stomach feels empty. I should've eaten something after this morning's adventures.

Despite me holding on to the handle above my head as the van rocks and bounces over the gravel road, I can't keep a firm grip and my elbow smacks into the window. I tuck my free hand under my leg to steady its shaking, but soon my foot is bouncing my leg up and down.

I stretch out, rest my head back, and try to relax. The cave is just a hole in the ground. I can do this. I *need* to do this. I close my eyes and suck in a deep breath slowly, exhaling even slower. Rachel and Vernon are probably watching me, but I don't care. I need to relax.

My eyes are still closed when we come to a stop. Even before I exit the car, I can feel the summer heat ruthlessly beating down on the mountainside, not that it matters with the way I'm feeling right now.

The cave will offer an escape from the sun, I tell myself, knowing fully-well that it won't work. The underlying fear I have of this place is more powerful.

Something bad happened here.

"You okay?" Rachel asks me quietly.

I open my eyes and realize I'm the only one still sitting in the van.

Perry opens the back of the van and rifles through everything they brought. "You don't have to come in with us if you're not comfortable."

I shake my head. "No, you won't get accurate data if we don't check out the specific place I woke up."

As they pull out what they need from the van, I stand next to Vernon at the edge of the path and look out across the valley. Even though I'm up higher than the towers downtown, I feel safer in this direction with the cave behind me.

After a minute, Vernon points at the mountain on the opposite side of the city.

"We were over there during your first week," he says. "You see that break in the trees? That's where we were."

There are several breaks in the trees, but I don't feel like talking much so I nod.

"We're lucky to live in a place with such natural beauty."

Another nod. The city's beauty—and even Vernon's words—are only barely a blip on my radar.

"I'm sorry for what happened at the dinner party," Vernon

says. "I stopped by ESTR the next day, but you weren't there. Rachel said you were okay, though, which I was glad to hear."

I watch as a pair of birds soar over the valley.

"I've been texting both Rachel and Perry all week, trying to get in touch with you, but you've been busy," he goes on.

I'm sweating, but I don't move to the shade near the cave opening. The leather Heat suit intensifies the sun's rays. Maybe my increased body temperature will remind me of what happened that gave me these abilities. It had to have been related to a fire or something. It's not natural.

"Ash, will you say something so I know you're not mad at me?"

I look over at him. "I'm not mad, Vernon. You helped me."

He gives me a sad smile. "Yeah, I guess I did, didn't I?"

"Your boss was, uh…"

He shakes his head. "Only trying to make sure you were okay. I overreacted. Actually, I'd love to have you stay at my house again if you want. Rachel says you've been staying at Perry's apartment and I know it's kind of small—"

"It's fine. I don't mind."

And I don't. Sure, I sleep on the couch, but I'm usually up at the same time as Perry anyway. Earlier, even, thanks to those lingering dreams of the cave, which I'm about to re-enter voluntarily. Besides, all week Perry and I have been training, so I haven't even missed my own private room at Vernon's. I wasn't ever really comfortable there anyway.

"Guys!" Perry calls behind us. "You ready?"

Rachel pulls on a stuffed backpack and buckles it across her chest and then at her waist.

"What's in there?" I ask.

"Food, water, extra lights, batteries, and some tools and containers in case we want to take samples," she says.

"We're prepared for anything." Perry pulls on a mask over his face and I watch as Rachel does the same.

"Make sure you have your Heat mask on," her muffled voice says. "Just in case there's any contaminants in the air. Vernon, you too."

Perry hands him one. Once we've all strapped on our air filters, Perry and Rachel start toward the cave. With heavy footsteps, I follow them in.

The shade from the cave offers immediate relief from the heat, but it only amplifies the goosebumps that prickle my skin under the leather. Despite the mask, the smell of lingering smoke grows stronger the further we walk, only reminding me more of the day I woke up here. My mind keeps going back to it. Waking up in the darkness. Feeling cold, confused, scared.

Once we reach a point where we have to click on our flashlights, I take the lead. My pace is slow and I try to put on a brave face and just march on without issue, but my feet simply won't *go*.

"We can come back later if you're not ready." Rachel puts a gentle hand on my shoulder.

I shake my head. "No, you were right. We have to do this now. The sooner we have answers, the better."

We step further into the cave. I don't know if it's the smell of the coal or the fact that I'm back here, but my brain flashes images into my consciousness. First, like a faint daydream, then with each passing step, the images appear clearer. One right after another at a rapid rate.

Walking out into the sunlight a few weeks ago.

The flashback of running into the smoking cave.

The feeling of my body slamming against the rocks when I first woke up.

Back and forth, over and over again, each scene passes by like snippets on a loop, bringing a sense of vertigo that makes me stop and double over, reaching out for someone—something—to steady me.

Someone behind me grasps my arm, but still I fall to the

rocky floor, my vision overcome with the flickering memories.

"Ash!" Perry calls to me.

I try to respond—I *want* to respond—but no words come out. My breathing becomes erratic and the blood seems to drain from my head.

"That's it, we're going back," Rachel declares.

"Wait," Vernon says from somewhere behind them. Closer, he asks, "Ash, are you okay?"

I feel my mask pulled up so my face is exposed and cool plastic presses against my lips.

"Here, drink," Perry says.

I try to focus my eyes on him, but it isn't until I drink something that my vision clears. "That helps." I'm relieved to hear my own voice.

"Drink more," Rachel urges, flashing her light up to the rocky ceiling.

I take the bottle from Perry and down half of it.

"Easy, dude. You don't want to hurl." He smiles so I know he's joking. I appreciate the humor to lighten up the mood.

My head is clearer now and I get back to my feet with the help of the guys. "I'm good."

"Are you sure?" Vernon keeps a loose grip on my arm.

"Yeah, let's go."

We move on, but after a few more steps, the visions return. Faster this time. *Much* faster.

Along with the visions comes the vertigo again and my steps become heavier, but still I press on. I think we're almost there. Just a little bit more.

My hands begin to shake again. The next minute, my head follows suit, building with a growing crescendo until I can't control any part of me anymore. I feel someone's hand on my back, but it only throws my balance off and I crash to the rocky floor, shaking uncontrollably.

My head explodes with pain. I can't tell if it's from the fall, the shakes, or the visions. It's hard to determine since my eyesight is gone. Replaced instead by swirls of color. Reds, oranges, yellows. Even glimpses of black.

I try to follow the movement with my eyes, but I can't focus on which way is up or down, where the bursts of color are coming from. I'm lost in a void of confusion, swirling into an abyss I can't be certain is my imagination.

"Ash!" Someone calls from a distance. Or maybe it's right next to me? I can't tell.

The voice doesn't even sound familiar to me anymore.

Who is it?

Where are they?

Do *they* know what happened to me in here? Why I fear it so much?

Are they someone I should fear?

I would run, but I can't feel my feet, my legs. I'm not even sure I'm a part of my body anymore.

Maybe my soul has escaped.

Maybe I'm lost in the ether.

Maybe none of it ever existed.

Maybe it was all a dream.

Chapter Seventeen

The heat is what I notice first. The rising temperature of my body. The distinct feeling of the sun beating down on me. The same feeling I had just before we entered—

The cave.

My eyes snap open, but the light is too bright and I immediately close them. Still, I start to sit up.

"Whoa, easy," Vernon says. The sun is momentarily blocked out and when I squint my eyes again, the details of his face begin to come into focus as my vision adjusts to the light. "You scared us."

I look around. We're outside the cave, behind the van so it blocks most of the sun. "Where's Rachel and Perry?"

He puts his hand on my shoulder to steady me. "They're right here."

Suddenly, I'm pulled into a tight hug from behind.

"I'm so glad you're okay!" Rachel releases her hold and comes around to look at me. She kneels next to me. Perry crouches behind her, inspecting me as well. All three of them help to further block out the sunlight.

"Ash, I'm so sorry," she goes on. "I shouldn't have pushed you to keep going like that. It was obvious you weren't ready. I should've been tracking your vitals and—"

"It's okay," I say. "What happened?"

"You had a seizure," Perry says.

"That's my best guess, anyway," Rachel clarifies.

"We carried you out as fast as we could," Vernon adds.

"So you didn't find much?"

Rachel shakes her head. "It doesn't matter. I'm just glad you're okay."

My head is still foggy from whatever happened inside. "No, it's not okay. That's why we came here."

"We can come back later."

"No, we're here now," I push. "This is what we came for. You know the way. The cave doesn't affect you like it does me. Go, get some samples or whatever you're going to do, and bring it back to the lab so we can start to piece together my history."

Rachel and Perry look at each other.

"I'll stay out here with Vernon," I say.

Perry gives me a nervous look.

"Guys, I'll be okay." We have work to do, even if I can't be a part of it.

Rachel rises to her feet and nods away from me. Perry follows her around the front of the van and I hear their low murmuring voices, but can't quite make out what they're saying. Instead, I sit up and look out toward the valley, relishing in the faint breeze that relieves a tiny bit of the sun's warmth.

"Okay, we'll make a quick trip in," Rachel says when they return.

Perry lifts his pack up onto his back and buckles it across his chest and his waist.

"Vernon, do you mind sitting with him?" she asks.

Chapter Seventeen

"Yeah, no problem," he says quickly.

She steps over to Perry, who hands her a flashlight. "We'll try to hurry."

"Just make sure you get everything you need," I say. "I don't want to have to come back here."

Perry grabs his flashlight and turns to Rachel. "Ready?"

She turns back to me. "Are you sure you're okay with this?"

"I'll be fine," I assure her. "You guys go. Otherwise, this will have been a wasted trip."

With another nervous glance, Rachel and Perry venture back into the cave. I watch them until they disappear into the darkness, hoping I haven't just sent them on a suicide trip.

"They'll be okay," Vernon says from behind me.

Startled, I turn and look at him, taking a moment to fully process what he said.

"Huh? Oh, yeah. I hope so."

"They're smart, too," he adds. "If they feel like something is off they'll turn around."

Like I should have.

"Yeah," I murmur.

"Do you need anything?" he asks. "Want me to start the van so you can sit in the AC?"

"No, but I could use some water."

His face lights up. "Water? Sure! Yeah, I'll get that for you. Don't move."

I watch as he disappears around the other side of the van, likely searching the driver's seat for the stash of reserves that Perry brought with us.

I hope whatever caused me to have a seizure in the cave doesn't have any harmful effects on Rachel and Perry. Then again, they're the researchers, so if they thought something was in the air, they wouldn't have gone back in.

It just makes me wonder if I'm even cut out to use my powers to help others. How do I know that something else won't cause another seizure for me? Or worse? You can't plan for something unexpected like that.

With the threat of Black Magnet—and especially the Gatekeeper—I need to be on top of things in order to help people. I need to know how my body will react in certain situations.

And how did things get so complicated so quickly? A part of me feels like I just showed up and am now intruding on the lives of Rachel, Perry, and Vernon. But I guess Rachel's curious about the world, so she's made it her mission to understand me and my extraordinary abilities. And while Perry shares the same interest, he's more infatuated with the possibilities of what my powers could do—namely, fight "bad guys," as he's said on more than one occasion during our training sessions.

But Vernon's right. They're smart people so they're not going to get into anything they suspect might be too dangerous.

Pausing, I listen for the sound of Vernon rummaging through the van, but instead I hear quick footsteps on the ground. Multiple footsteps.

Jumping to my feet, I pull the mask back over my head and move around the back side of the van, opposite where the footsteps are. I peek in the windows to look for Vernon, but don't see him. Where the hell did he go?

"Holy shit, it's hot," someone says from the front of the van.

"Shh! He's gotta be here somewhere," another one says.

They're close. Too close.

I hear the distinct sound of a gun loading and contemplate my next move. My shadow stretches out next to the van's toward the valley. If I don't move, my shadow blends in with the van's. I don't know how much time I have before they spot me—

"Hey!" One of them dressed in black from head-to-toe shouts at me as he comes along the back of the van. He seems just as startled as I am and takes an extra second to raise his gun.

I knock it out of his grip with my arm and throw a punch at him that misses. Perry might be pushing me to learn my abilities, but my hand-to-hand fighting is lacking. I make a mental note to work on that.

The other two men run up and fire at nothing in particular. This is getting too close and they have me outnumbered, so I burst into flame and fly into the air. Their pistols won't be able to hit anything with accuracy this far away. I just need to move quick and attack from afar.

Back flipping a couple times, I swoop down and drive my burning fist into the gut of the unarmed thug. In an instant, I increase my body heat and rise higher into the clear blue sky.

Gunshots fire from behind the van and I hear bullets fly by me. Opening my palm down toward them, I fire a quick fireball in their direction, watching them scatter into the trees beyond the path.

I chance another fly-by, trying to determine where they're hiding. Once I land, I hear another gunshot and fire off a steady stream of flame in the direction of the sound. As the heat blasts, I feel the light impact of the nearly-melted bullet on my chest.

When the flames dissipate, I listen closely for any more attacks. Instead, all I hear is the first thug moaning on the ground as he clutches his stomach.

"You're just going to hide out after you sought me out?" I yell into the trees.

Nothing. The only sound is my voice echoing into the wind. Except—

Clanging. Screeching. Metal on metal. It grows louder and louder. I turn just in time to see Black Magnet pull himself up from the cliff by the valley.

Quickly, I extend two hands toward him and throw fire in his direction, but I immediately feel an arm around my neck and I'm pulled back to the ground.

The thug on the ground must've been faking it.

"What do you want?" I bark, swinging my arms as I hear

the other two thugs approach and restrain me. One of them holds a gun to my head.

Black Magnet raises his arm up and a jagged piece of shrapnel extends out like a bayonet. I catch a glimpse in his eyes through the metal. They look sad, almost remorseful.

Still, he pulls back his arm and prepares to swing it at me.

Panicking, I burst into flames again. The weight of the three thugs is enough to keep me grounded, but the fire covering my body forces each of them to release their grip.

Black Magnet doesn't stop his attack, though. Once free from the restraints of the thugs, I fly up into the air and away from the attack, barely missing the metal skewer.

"Darryl, are you all right?" one of them cries out from below.

The other one shouts, "Hey, that's not how this was supposed to go!"

The third thug, the one who first attacked me, clutches at his bleeding stomach on the ground with the shrapnel piece sticking out of it.

The other two grab ahold of their buddy and start dragging him down the path that leads back into the city. A futile attempt to get him to help. If I didn't need to ignite every time I flew, I could get him to a hospital faster.

Pissed, I land hard in the blood stain on the ground where the man was stabbed and face Black Magnet.

"What the hell do you want with me?" I shout.

He doesn't say anything. Doesn't move. Just stares. That only fuels my anger.

"You likely just killed someone and you don't have any reason to give for his death?"

Finally, Black Magnet steps forward. Another piece of shrapnel extends from his arm. The screeching sound of metal scraping metal grows louder as he picks up his pace.

I wait for him to get into position before igniting once again in flame and launching directly at him. Hooking my arms around his waist as I fly into him, I pin him hard against the van, allowing the rage to fuel my body, increasing my heat index to a rate higher than I've ever reached before.

Metal falls around me as he's demagnetized, but I hold my position, pinning him against the van as pieces of Black Magnet's armor begin to fuse with the metal panels of the vehicle.

"What's going on?" Perry's voice breaks my concentration, giving Black Magnet an opportunity to push me away.

I fall to the ground, quickly turning so I can get a good look at who Black Magnet really is. Only, the metal covering his face appears to be a helmet of sorts, which conceals the man's face. Still, I notice that his arms and torso are badly burned from my attack.

Moments later, he remagnetizes and the metal pieces that fused with the van struggles to reattach to him. Finally, the whole side panel of the vehicle detaches and wraps around Black Magnet, who runs to the side of the cliff and jumps. I sit up to follow, but my vision goes black with lightheadedness and my knees give out as soon as I get to my feet.

"My van!" Perry shouts.

"Ash, are you okay?" Rachel calls.

I don't answer right away, still trying to figure out what just happened, and wondering where the hell Vernon went.

Chapter Eighteen

Rachel rushes to me and helps me sit up. Perry runs to the edge and looks over.

"Are you hurt?" she asks. "Should we call an ambulance?"

"Not really." I watch Perry, hoping he'll come back with a lead of where Black Magnet might've went.

"Are you sure?" she pushes.

"Yeah, just tired."

Perry comes back over and crouches beside us.

"Anything?" I ask.

He shakes his head. "Nothing. I thought I saw some of the trees move, but that was just a bird."

"Damn it."

"We'll find him, Ash," Rachel says encouragingly.

"He *killed* someone, Rach," I say. "Right in front of me."

Neither of them say anything.

How could I have let him get away? Especially after he killed someone who was helping him. I wonder how many other people Black Magnet has killed. I'm going to make him pay.

"Where's Vernon?" Rachel finally breaks the silence.

"I don't know," I say. "He said he was going to get me some water and the next thing I knew, the thugs showed up."

Perry and Rachel exchange worried glances.

"I'll call him." Perry rises to his feet and steps away from us as he brings his phone to his ear.

"Ash, what exactly happened?" Rachel asks.

"I'll tell you as soon as we find Vernon," I say. "Maybe he can help me piece together what I didn't see."

Perry comes back over. "He's almost back down to the lab. He said he heard the thugs coming up the path when he went to get water and hid. Once the attack started, he wanted to be out of the way so there weren't any distractions. But when the thugs were on their way back down with their injured friend, he helped them carry him."

He did all that without telling me? And why would he run and hide when the farthest he needed to go was the other side of the van to get me water? He knew what I went through in the cave. He should've warned me.

Something's not adding up, but I don't say anything. I can't accuse a friend until I have more solid proof.

"We should go back down too," Rachel says quietly. "Do you think that's drivable?"

Perry sighs and glances at the damaged van with the side panel missing and the concave sliding door. "I can give it a shot, but my best guess would be that we're going to need to hike it."

"Well, see what you can do." She turns to me. "Do you think you'll be okay on your feet?"

I smirk. "I can try, but I still never got that water."

She rolls her eyes and smiles back. "You're annoying."

Getting up, she goes around to the back of the van while Perry tries to get it running from the driver's seat. The engine groans, but refuses to start. When Rachel hands me the bottle of water, Perry's curse words drown out my thanks.

"I'm going to take that as not a good sign," she says when he comes back around

"No, I think there's a leak somewhere underneath," he says. "Not to mention, even if I *could* get it started, the panels are so bent to shit that they're rubbing on the tires. I'm not sure we'd even make it very far before one of them popped."

I finish sucking down half of the bottle and ask breathlessly, "So we're walking then?"

"Can you manage?" he asks.

"I should be fine. Can we carry everything?"

He rocks his head back and forth. "I think so."

"All right, then let's load up," Rachel says.

They pull out the bags they wore into the cave and find another one that I can wear. Even though I tell them I can carry more in mine, they still make sure the one on my back is lighter. The fight with Black Magnet has left me tired, sure, but it feels more like I've had a strenuous workout, not that I've just had open-heart surgery.

"I hope that guy who got hurt is okay," Rachel murmurs as we head back toward the city. I try not to notice the steady trail of blood, but I'm sure it's what sparked her comment.

"His friends started bringing him down almost as soon as it happened," I say.

"And Vernon says he helped," Perry adds.

"Yeah, but it's still a shame," she says. "Was it clear what they were there for?"

I shake my head. "Not really. Well, I mean, it was clear they were after *me*, but I'm not sure why."

"Maybe Black Magnet hired him," Perry suggests. "Was he there before or after the thugs?"

"After."

"And did they stick around when he attacked?"

Chapter Eighteen

"Yeah."

I think about how the one got stabbed. He was trying to restrain me but I got away before I was the victim. It was clear they weren't afraid of Black Magnet—at least, not afraid that he'd attack them in that instant. Once he did—even if it was accidental—they took off. Can't say I blame them.

"I'm willing to bet they were working together," Perry says.

"You think someone would take to a guy in a getup like that seriously?" Rachel asks, then quickly adds, "No offense, Ash."

"There's a person under all of that metal," I say. "Maybe he approached them without any of that on. We need to talk to Vernon."

"Vernon?" Rachel asks. "How would he know if Black Magnet hired them?"

"I was thinking that too, actually," Perry says. "He must've seen more than Ash, but it doesn't make sense because why wouldn't he warn you?"

"I don't know," I say.

"I'm sure there's a perfectly good reason," Rachel says, unsure of herself.

"Maybe," I murmur.

"I wonder what he has against you, though," Perry says. "Black Magnet, that is. Heat hasn't been around that long to make very many enemies. At least, I don't think."

"He has had his fair share of fights, though," Rachel adds.

"You think I made enemies in that time?" I ask.

"It's possible," Perry says. "It's just even more reason to figure out why Black Magnet is coming after you."

"Maybe it's all a planned effort," Rachel says. "There's a huge organized crime problem in Olympia. Could be happening here too."

"I don't know," I mutter. "I'd rather not worry about all of that right now."

"But Ash, there's someone who's coming after you," Perry

pushes. "We don't know whether he wants to kidnap you, kill you, or just hurt you—"

"He wants to kill me. Look what happened to his hired help."

"Even more reason to worry about this now!" he pushes.

"Okay, okay," Rachel says. "We'll talk about it more at the lab, but let's just…talk about something else. Or nothing else."

Nothing else seems to suit us best because soon the only sound is our feet on the blood-stained gravel.

By the time we get down to ESTR in the city, Vernon is stepping out of a white beat-up sedan. Definitely not his slick-black ride.

"Who's car is that?" I ask.

"Must be an Uber," Rachel says. After the car drives away, she runs to Vernon and hugs him. "You're okay! They didn't hurt you, did they?"

"Those guys?" He shakes his head. "No. They were too scared for their friend."

Perry narrows his eyes. "But they're criminals. I mean, they hiked up that mountain to attack Ash—Heat—but a stranger jumping out of the woods doesn't startle them?"

"I didn't really jump out…"

"Yeah, and I'm sure everyone was most concerned about their friend who was dying," Rachel adds. "How's he doing?"

Vernon shakes his head. "He didn't make it."

I let out a deep breath and we're all quiet as we process how our simple exploration trip turned deadly.

Finally, Rachel nods to the door. "Come on, let's get inside where we can all sit down and talk about everything. We all have questions and I think it's important for everyone to be on the same page."

Inside, Perry, Rachel, and I drop our things on a free work table. I roll my head to try to loosen up the muscles in my neck. The whole place is still quiet. Definitely a good thing after what just happened at the top of the mountain.

Chapter Eighteen

We each take a seat. Vernon tugs the sleeves of his green hoodie so they're covering his hands and I sit across from his and cross my arms. Rachel and Perry dig through the bags we brought down until they retrieve the samples they took from the cave.

"Ash, you should get another glass of water." Rachel stacks several sealed containers of rock fragments on a metal lab table.

"I'm fine." I probably *could* use some water, but right now I want answers more than a wet whistle.

"Water will do you some good," she says, but doesn't push it further.

Instead, she works at her computer, tapping away at the keyboard and fussing with one of the containers. I don't pay too close attention, opting to keep my eyes on Vernon instead.

Once the rest of the samples are unloaded, Perry takes a seat at his desk and leans on his hands. Rachel continues to putz at her desk, but I decide I can't wait any longer.

"So what happened?" I ask Vernon.

"There was an attack. You didn't notice?" He smiles to try to lighten the mood, but I don't return it. Sensing my tone, he continues more seriously, "When I went to get you the water, I heard footsteps. Several of them, so I knew there would be trouble."

"And you just left Ash there?" Perry asks.

"I didn't think I had enough time to warn him and get to safety," he says. "I figured since he has his powers, he's better equipped to fight them off than I was."

"But you still just left him," Perry pushes. "Without warning."

Vernon shrugs and winces. "It was poor judgment on my part and for that I apologize, Ash."

"What's the matter?" Rachel asks him, noticing his pain. "Are you hurt? What happened?"

"Nothing," he says quickly. "I just pinched a nerve."

I narrow my eyes but still don't say anything.

"So what happened after you hid?" Perry asks.

"I watched until Black Magnet showed up and that man was stabbed," he says. "When I noticed the group of men started carrying their friend down the path, I decided to follow them."

"How did you get roped into helping them?" Perry asks.

"I noticed that one of them was bleeding pretty badly and I asked them if they wanted help."

Finally, I break my silence. "So you ran away from them when they first showed up because you thought they'd attack us, but you didn't think anything of jumping out of the woods at them?"

"I told you, I didn't *jump out* at them…"

"Then how exactly did it go?" I push. "Because to me, if my friend was just attacked and I was worried about his life, I would be more than a little jumpy if a stranger showed up out of nowhere and offered to help."

"Ash," Rachel warns.

Vernon looks down at his sleeve again. "No, it's okay. I get it. It looks weird. But I'm asking you to trust me."

"We do," she says quickly. "We're just trying to figure out what happened and why."

He nods. "Those are questions I'd like to know the answers to as well."

"Would you?" I ask.

He looks up at me, perplexed. "Of course."

"So you're being completely honest?"

"Ash," Rachel warns again. Louder this time.

"What are you trying to say?" Vernon asks.

"What's with the hoodie?"

Perry seems to just notice it. "Yeah, it's like eighty-five degrees out. You didn't have it on before."

Vernon pulls the sleeves over his hands completely. "Oh. The air conditioning is cold in here."

"You had it on when you got out of the cab, too."

Chapter Eighteen

"Ash, what difference does it make?" Rachel asks.

"I just want him to answer the question."

"Can't a guy just wear a sweatshirt?" His lip twitches up in a slight smirk and that sets me off.

Before I realize it, I'm jumping on him. The chair tumbles backward onto the floor and we both fall. Holding my grip, I struggle with him until I pin him down.

"*Ash, what are you doing!*" Rachel shouts from behind me.

Vaguely, I notice Perry reaching for me in an attempt to pull me away, but my complete concentration is on seeing what Vernon's hiding under his sweatshirt.

He pushes me away a few times until he launches into an all-out assault, throwing punches that hit my shoulders, sides, and even one in my ear, which makes it ring.

After a minute, Perry wraps both of his arms around my waist and heaves me off of Vernon. All four of us stare at each other. The men all breathing heavily and Rachel staring between me and Vernon in disbelief.

"*What the hell was that?*" she shouts. "Ash, that was completely—"

"Look!" I point at Vernon just as he's tucking his sweatshirt back down over his red and inflamed skin.

Burns.

Rachel's anger with me seems to dissipate when she notices Vernon's injuries. "What happened? You said you weren't hurt."

He rises to his feet and tugs the sleeves of his sweatshirt lower, even though he's already covered. "Nothing. This was just…it was just, uh, small grease fire at the house."

Perry gets up and says, "Pull up your sleeves."

"No." He's stern, his voice now devoid of any kindness.

"You have burns all over you," I say. "Just like what Heat gave to Black Magnet up by the cave."

I can feel everyone's eyes on me as I lay out the accusation that's been churning in my mind for a while now.

"Ash…" Rachel says softly.

"You don't know what you're talking about." Vernon turns to the door. "I didn't come here to be attacked. I came here to make sure the rest of you were okay after what happened at the top of that mountain."

"You mean when you attacked us as Black Magnet?" I ask.

"That's not—you're *way* off base here!"

"Tell us the truth, then."

He glares at me with gritted teeth. Finally, he turns and walks out. I step forward to chase after him, but Perry holds me back.

"Not right now," he says. "If he's really Black Magnet, we're not done with him."

Chapter Nineteen

So...that just happened, huh?" Perry asks after neither me nor Rachel say anything else.

"Where did that come from?" Rachel asks quietly.

"He's never been around when Black Magnet showed up, but he always seemed to have an alibi," I say. "This time was just too far-fetched. I'm sorry. I know you guys wanted to believe what he said was true because he's your friend, but—"

"You're our friend too," she says.

"He probably thought he'd be able to kill you and then act all sad when we saw," Perry says.

"I just don't know how he could do that." She sniffles and her voice breaks. "He's always been our friend."

"I know," I say with a nod. "He's been very generous with me, too. Which makes me wonder if he's being put up to it."

"What do you mean?" She wipes at her eyes.

"Well, you mentioned that there's an organized crime problem in Olympia and it made me wonder if we have something similar here," I explain.

"You think there are mobsters in Ellsworth?" Perry asks in disbelief.

"No, but I think that someone wants me dead. Or out of the way somehow. Maybe they found out somehow that Vernon knew me and threatened him to get his hands dirty instead."

"By who, though?" Rachel asks.

"The Gatekeeper?" I shrug. "Or maybe someone else. I don't know. The bigger question I have is *why*. Like Perry said, I haven't been in Ellsworth that long to have gained an enemy who wants to kill me."

"Well, obviously someone does," she says. "And they've hired Vernon to do it for them." She leans against the nearest desk and rubs her temples. "Ugh, I just feel so stupid to not have seen it."

"None of us did." Perry steps over to her and rubs her back. "The important thing is that now we know and we can move forward."

One of the computers from across the room makes an alert sound and Rachel rushes to it. Perry and I follow.

"The toxicity tests are done," she says.

"You've already started running tests on the samples?" I ask.

"Yeah, when you were brooding over Vernon," she says.

"And with good reason." Perry waves a finger at me. "Your instincts were right on with him. That's good."

I can't help but smile at his praise. In an effort to hide it, though, I clear my throat and ask Rachel, "I thought you already ran those before we went in?"

"These are more accurate," she says. "Taken right from the source."

"What's it say?"

"Nothing surprising." Perry leans over her shoulder to read the computer screen. "High levels of arsenic, lead, mercury."

"Arsenic?" I blurt.

Chapter Nineteen

"All three have high atomic weights," Perry murmurs to her, ignoring me.

"We'll have to keep an eye on each of us to make sure we don't experience nausea, numbness, or vomiting," she adds. "I don't feel anything, do you?"

"Like a headache or weakness, right?" he asks.

She nods. "Achy joints and muscles, that sort of thing."

He shakes his head. "Nothing like that, but we went into the cave with masks on, so I'm sure that helped. The only one who was really fully exposed to it was Ash."

Finally, they both turn to me.

"What are you guys talking about?" I ask.

"Do you feel weak at all?" Rachel asks.

I shrug. "I mean, I *did* just fight off some thugs at the top of the mountain—oh, and Black Magnet too. All after I had that seizure. That's not to mention the hike *down* the mountain and my scuffle with Vernon."

She narrows her eyes. "Hmm, he's right. He wouldn't be able to do all of that if he was experiencing any level of poisoning."

"Poisoning? Guys, what's going on?"

"Well, the toxicity levels in the samples are high," Perry explains.

Rachel scrolls through the results some more. "The mercury levels are *really* high."

"What does that mean?" I ask.

Perry rocks his head back and forth. "Well, depending on how long you were exposed, there's a chance you could be experiencing some of the side effects we were asking you about, maybe even worse."

"You're talking about my time in the cave before I met you guys, right?"

He nods.

"If I was poisoned, the symptoms would've already shown themselves by now," I say. "Wouldn't they?"

He shoots me a look. “Ash, you can light things on fire with your hands. That’s not normal!”

I smirk. “Oh. Right. But do you really think what you found could cause my abilities?”

“I don’t know,” Rachel says. “I mean, we determined that you weren’t in the cave for long because of lack of facial hair and there being no sign of malnourishment, but since you can’t remember it’s hard to say. I would still like to take another sample of your blood. See if there are any signs of the toxins in there.”

“Didn’t you do that before?” I ask.

“I did, but I wasn’t really sure what I was looking for. Now I do. Actually, I should sample all of our blood, just to be safe.”

She gets up and grabs a small bag of supplies from the medic room.

“You first, Ash,” she says. “Just a little sample.”

Cringing, I take a seat in a chair. She wraps a rubber band around my bicep and wipes a spot on the inside of my elbow with alcohol. After a few flicks of her finger against the spot she wiped, she sticks the needle in and fills several vials with my blood. When she pulls it out, she quickly presses down on the spot with a patch of gauze.

“Easy enough, right?” She shakes the vials as she carries them to a work table by the wall.

“*Just a little sample?*” I press the gauze tight to my arm and raise it. “You must’ve taken a pint!”

“Dude, why are you whining?” Perry asks. “Relax.”

I suck in a deep breath and check to see if the bleeding’s stopped. It has.

Perry gets up and searches through Rachel’s supply bag until he finds the Band-Aids.

“You want a princess Band-Aid for that?” he asks with a snicker.

I ignore him. “What does the sample show?”

“It’s too soon to tell just yet,” Rachel says over her shoulder from her work table. "We need to let it sit for a minute or two. Perry, you're up."

She takes the same amount of blood from him and I relish in the fact that he winces at the prick too. Then he and Rachel swap and he takes a sample from her.

After everyone's all bandaged up, Rachel takes a seat at her work table again and shakes some of the vials of blood and sets them back in front of their post-it labels identifying who they belong to.

"What are we waiting for?" I ask.

She turns and leans back in her chair. "I've added some compounds to the blood that'll tell me whether you've been exposed to some of the toxins found in the cave. This isn't the most foolproof test because we're more of a tech lab than a bio lab, but it'll do for now."

"So...we just wait until the results are ready?" I ask.

"Why don't you tell us what happened when we were in the cave," Rachel says. "The first time with all of us."

That seems like so long ago, but still what I experienced comes back to me easily. "I just saw...colors. I felt disoriented, too. But all I really saw were splotches of colors." I shake away the memory. "I didn't like it."

"It didn't look like you did," Perry says.

"Do you think it was a flashback?" Rachel asks.

"Of what?" Perry asks.

"Well, sometimes people just see colors and feel emotions in their dreams," she explains. "Ash could've been experiencing a flashback to an emotion he either felt in the cave or one that he associates with his time in there."

"No, I don't think it was a memory," I say. "But it did feel—I don't know—familiar maybe? Like I've experienced something like that before. I don't know. I don't remember."

Perry looks over at her. "Do you think it could have something to do with the exposure levels?"

She scrunches her face. "Maybe. But he's been out of the cave for two weeks and he's still having flashbacks. Poisoning like this wouldn't result in any sort of memory loss. Confusion, maybe, but even if that were the case he'd be able to recall his memories with a few prompts."

"Has it been long enough yet?" I ask. "What does my blood show?"

She turns and looks at the samples. "No arsenic, no lead…"

"What?" I ask.

Perry comes up behind her and looks at the result. "Whoa."

"Guys, that's not helping. What is it?"

"Okay, I don't want you to freak out or anything, but this shows that the mercury levels in your blood are *really* high," Rachel says. She lowers her voice and mutters to herself, "Well, the mercury in the cave was really high too, so maybe that's to be expected…"

"What does that mean?" I ask.

Perry shakes his head. "But look at our samples. They have normal levels. Actually, they're significantly lower than Ash's."

"So it's not likely that this spike is from his entry into the cave today," she says.

"No, it must be from two weeks ago."

"But that doesn't make sense," she counters. "It'd be out of his system by now and if it wasn't, he'd be showing some other symptoms from it."

"Can you say *superpowers*?" he asks.

"Hmm, maybe. I mean, mercury tends to affect the body's nervous system," she says to him.

"Yeah, and his nerves would have had to have adjusted because otherwise his body wouldn't be able to withstand the level of heat he experiences when he's using his powers—especially for a prolonged period of time."

"Guys." I try to break into their discussion, but they're gone on their train of thought.

Chapter Nineteen

"That's probably why he had a seizure in the cave," she explains. "He was re-exposed to the harmful chemicals, which brought up subconscious memories. It's both biological and psychological."

"You think the mercury is related to his amnesia?"

She shakes her head. "I'd have to do more tests to be sure. I don't think it's likely, but mercury poisoning *can* cause confusion. Besides, he's already proved that the unlikely is very much possible."

"So basically," I say loudly, forcing my way into their conversation, "you found out *how* I got my powers, but not how I ended up in the cave in the first place."

"All we know is what you remember," Rachel says.

Yeah, like that doesn't put a lot of pressure on me.

I don't say anything as I head toward the door.

"Where are you going?" Perry asks.

"For a walk. I need to think."

"Are you okay?" he asks. "You probably shouldn't be alone."

"I'll be fine!" I slip out into the hall and power walk to the exit before either of them can stop me.

FROM THE LAB, my footsteps carry me along a street that heads north. It's the same direction we've gone in to get out of the city for the mall with Rachel and the training field with Perry. Only, they've always ventured to the other side of the river to get on the expressway that snakes through downtown underground and shoots north out of the city. They both live on that side, so it makes sense.

But right now I want unfamiliar territory. You'd think that wouldn't be so hard for me to find, but even in the two weeks since I've been here, I've had a good amount of lasting memories with people I consider my friends. This part of town is one area

I haven't explored by car, let alone on foot.

Actually, I haven't ventured too much in the city at all. There was that Ellsworth tour with Vernon when I first woke up, but definitely never on my own. Yet the city feels familiar. The streets are laid out in a simple grid and I anticipate each street name before I can even make out what the sign reads.

Somehow, instinctively, I *know* that there's a giant warehouse on the corner of Second Street and Chestnut Avenue. I know that once you cross Third Street, the area turns from industrial to residential. Originally housing for the immigrants who worked at the plants that harnessed the power of the river. I know that if I were one street over, I'd be walking along a commercial street with small shops and restaurants packed together.

Obviously, it gets easier to determine the street pattern once I get north of downtown and the streets running east and west are numbered in ascending order. But it's more than that. Landmarks are familiar too. The way the sidewalk curves around the trees on Chestnut Avenue, the signs pointing to Riverside Park several streets over, the shadows the mountains cast as the day draws to a close.

Rachel and Perry might not have been able to tell me *how* I ended up in the cave or even who I was before that, but I can be certain of one thing: Ellsworth is, and has always been, my home. I can feel it deep in my gut.

This neighborhood in particular rekindles a sense of belonging in me I haven't ever felt before. It's as if I'm walking closer to something that I know better than anything else. Excitement builds as I march forward. With each step, hopefully walking closer to home.

It's dusk and I stop every so often to really get a good look at the houses on the street, but once I see them with my eyes, I can see them in my head too. The way the street looks in the fall, with the leaves collected along the curb. Or even houses and other buildings that used to stand tall before they were torn down for one reason or another.

My mind is slowly remembering a vivid memory. This time, though, it's nothing like the intense headaches I'd get with the flashbacks, but it's still a memory nonetheless. It's so ingrained in me that it takes almost no effort to come to the surface. Like a fuzzy picture slowly focusing.

Number 894 Chestnut Avenue. That address seems significant. Maybe it's my address. Or maybe that girl I saw in my flashbacks. Of course, that might too obvious. Why would I know her address better than my own? Either way, I can tell I'm close.

I look up at the house I've stopped in front of. A narrow two-story structure that has a deep lot and a skinny alley behind it that hides the garages from the street. I can't see it from where I'm standing at the front, but I know the alley is there. I can almost picture myself playing basketball back there. I wonder if that's just wishful thinking, though.

Still, the house seems familiar, albeit a little different than what I think I remember. The number over the front door reads 873.

I'm really close.

Crossing the street, I follow the numbers as they ascend with each house I pass.

886.

888.

890.

892.

Here!

Number 894 is a modest two-story freestanding powder blue house with a wide front porch and black shutters on the upper windows. It brings back a whole flood of memories.

Sitting on the front porch in the mornings.

The squeaky front steps.

Climbing on the porch roof to get a better view of the Fourth of July fireworks shot off at Riverside Park.

Even before I step foot inside, I can picture the crown moulding, the finish worn off of the stairs banister from so much use, even the slanted ceiling in the bathroom from the roofline.

This is my home. And I'm standing right in front of it.

My family is inside.

My heart rate picks up. My palms suddenly become sweaty. This is it. This it the moment I've been waiting for since I woke up in the cave. But important questions still ring in my mind and make me hesitate.

Have they already given up on finding me? Or are they still deep in their search? Maybe once I see them all of my other memories will come flooding back too. Maybe this is the answer I've been looking for.

I run up the front steps—noting that they don't creak like they used to. It doesn't matter. This porch, with the swing on the right and the intricate woodwork framing the door, is familiar.

Out of habit, I grab the doorknob, but stop myself. The lights are on inside, so someone must be home, but I can't remember *who*, exactly. I can picture my parents—my mother with her long blonde hair pulled back in a ponytail, my nearly-bald father. Both of them always came home from work filthy, their coveralls filled with dirt and grime.

I picture the reunion. My mother rushing through the door and wrapping me in a hug with tears in her eyes. My father embracing us both.

And I have a brother! I can't believe I forgot about him! Yes, the boy from my flashback is here too, I'm sure. Of course, he's likely grown up now, like I am. I can't wait for the whole family to pile out and welcome me home.

An involuntary smile spreads across my face as I knock three times.

A minute later, an older woman answers the door. She's shorter than I pictured—certainly nothing like the way I remember my family and she doesn't trigger any sort of memory from me—but she seems nice enough. Maybe she's a neighbor I don't remember.

"Can I help you?" She rests her hand against the door, partway closed.

My smile falters. I wasn't planning on this. I didn't think I'd have to say anything. I thought once she saw me, she'd recognize me and the reunion would take over from there.

"It's me."

Maybe she can't see me in the dark. I take half a step forward, but she backs away and closes the door a bit more.

"Ash?" I offer.

She shakes her head. "I'm sorry, I don't know who you are."

"But I think I live here."

"I'm afraid you're mistaken." The door closes a bit more. "I would appreciate it if you please left me alone."

My heart sinks and I step back.

I'm scaring her. The worst part is that even though I know this house in and out, this woman is a complete stranger to me. Something's wrong.

"Sorry," I murmur, but she shuts the door without another word.

Slowly, I make my way down the steps and back toward the lab. Maybe the only people I know in this city are the ones I needed a break from. The ones who made me feel like a science experiment earlier.

I wish I had a place to go where I could forget about being Heat. About waking up in the cave. About not being able to remember. I'm no closer to figuring out who I am and instead I just feel stuck.

Chapter Twenty

We're lying in the grass after class, waiting for the evening football game to begin. We're together. Her leaning against a tree trunk, my head resting on her leg, our hands intertwined.

I gaze up into those eyes as she smiles down at me. She's beautiful. Funny. Smart.

"Oh, so you think you've got our future all planned out, don't you?" she asks with a chuckle.

"Of course! When I graduate I'll get a job and we'll save up until we can buy a house," I say. "Maybe one of those new ones over on Pine Avenue, near the mountains."

She laughs again. "It'll just be that easy, huh?"

"Hey, the hard part is already over," I say. "We've already found the person we're going to spend the rest of our lives with. Now we just need to find a place to live."

"Oh, is that all?"

I'm completely in love with this woman. She's strong, kind, intelligent, just all around good. The kind of woman who would make an excellent partner for anything we venture into.

Next thing I know, she's leaning down and kissing me. Feeling her soft lips against mine brings back feelings I haven't thought about since—

My body begins to shake and the image and feeling of her blurs before completely slipping away.

"Ash, wake up."

My eyes snap open and I see Perry in a T-shirt and a pair of boxer shorts. Not quite the view I wanted to see after that dream. I wish I could go back to sleep and bring that girl back.

I groan and roll onto my back on his couch. "What time is it?"

"You have to get up." He continues to shake me.

I swat him off. "It's Sunday, just let me be."

"No, listen to me," he insists. "Black Magnet—or Vernon or whoever it is—is only three streets over setting houses on fire."

That draws my attention and I sit up. "What? Where?"

He pulls out his phone and shows me the alert. "This was posted five minutes ago, but so far the commenters on the post are already wondering if it's you—well, Heat. You have to do something. It's four in the morning. Most people are still sleeping. By the time the fire department gets there—"

I push him aside and get to my feet, making my way to my bag where my Heat suit is.

"How many houses are on fire?" I go into the bathroom and shout through the door as I change.

"Sounds like there's three of them," he says. "No word on how many of the families have gotten out."

I emerge from the bathroom as Heat. "Where exactly is it?"

"Near the corner of North Center and Second Streets," he says. "Use the window!"

I push back the blackout curtains and am surprised to see the sun is just starting to come up. I squint at the light, but open the window and step out onto the fire escape. A moment later, I've erupted into fire and am soaring through the air.

Perry wasn't kidding about it being so close. As soon as I've cleared the roof of his apartment building, I spot the flames a couple streets over.

When I land on the street, there's already a small crowd watching the flames rise higher. They're all dressed in their pajamas, some of them are crying. They jump when they see me and one of the men approaches me.

"Did you do this?" he barks.

"No, I'm here to stop it," I say. "Is everyone out?"

"Our house is clear." One of the women from the group comes over to the man and hooks an arm around his waist, clutching her bathrobe closed with the other hand. "Our neighbors back there are all safe too, but this last house…"

"I'm on it."

Turning, I race into the burning building through the front door. The heat is intense, but luckily I'm used to it by now. It's the smoke that's hard to see through. Luckily, Perry made some adjustments to my mask so it's able to filter the thick smoke better.

"Hello!" I call out. "Is there anybody here?"

Through the roar of the fire, I hear groaning from the staircase. The fire creeps along the wall, but hasn't made its way to the steps yet. Which is good, because a frail old woman has collapsed on them.

I rush over and scoop her into my arms. The movement wakes her.

"Upstairs," she mutters. "My grandson…"

"I'll get him, but I need to get you out first." Breaking into a run again, I carry her out to the other two families displaced by the fires. "Call for an ambulance!"

"They're already on their way," the man from earlier tells me.

In the fresh air my eyes begin to water and I realize I have no protection from the smoke other than my mask. But there's no time to make adjustments, so I run back into the house and up the stairs, opting not to further fuel the fire by flying.

At the top of the stairs, I spot four rooms. Only one of them has tile, which makes that the bathroom. I crouch down beneath the smoke and try to get a look inside any of the other rooms. If someone passed out from the smoke, they'd be on the floor.

The door to one of the bedrooms is closed and I stand to try to open it, but it won't budge. Sinking to the floor to give my mask a rest from the smoke, I pound my fist on the door and shout, "If you can, open up! I'm just trying to help!"

I don't expect a response and immediately start planning my next move. The only thing I can think to do—other than kicking in the door and potentially hitting whoever is on the other side—is to burn a small hole around the knob and push it open that way.

Placing my hand near the latch, I let a trickle of fire seep out until the door gives. I push it open the rest of the way, noting that a chair was wedged under the doorknob from inside.

The open door brings the smoke into the clean-air room and I spot a lump among the bedsheets.

Slowly, I reach down and shake whoever's under the covers and they immediately pull away. Relief washes over me and I crouch down and pull the covers away.

"Hey, I'm not here to hurt you. I'm just going to take you down to your grandma."

"Where is she?" he asks through sniffles. "I'm scared."

"I know, bud." I wave for him to come closer. "Just trust me and I'll take you to her."

"What about the stranger?"

"What stranger?"

"In the house! I saw him through the keyhole!"

That explains the chair behind the door. But I don't have time to question him further. Smoke is filling the room and the fire is only weakening the supports underneath us. I might be able to withstand the flames, but this kid certainly can't.

"I'll take care of him, but first I need to get you out of here," I say. "Wrap yourself in your blanket and I'll carry you down."

He covers his head again and I scoop him up and head back down the stairs. Before I get to the door, though, I'm hit from the side and tumble to the floor.

The boy screams and I send out a stream of fire in the direction of the hit.

"Run! Outside! Don't stop until you've reached your family!"

The boy untangles himself from the blanket and sprints out the door, which is luckily only a few feet away.

Turning, I try to locate my attacker, but can't see anything through the smoke. The good thing is, I have a mask to filter all of this while they're left breathing it all in.

At least I hope that's the case.

Another blow from the side sends me back to the floor and I spot a set of legs winding up to kick me. I throw a fireball his way and his pant leg catches on fire—likely dried out from the burning house.

I jump to my feet and charge in his direction, but despite swinging my arms around to hit him, I don't make contact with anything until I hit the burning wall. Debris flies in my face and I stumble backward, colliding into the man I saw under the smoke.

I must've startled him just as much as he startled me, because it takes a second for him to throw a punch my way. His fist grazes my ear and I drive mine into his chest.

Backing away, he hunches over into a coughing fit, unable to control it any longer. Even if he's attacking me—and likely started the fire if that little boy's account has any merit—I still need to get him out of here into some fresh air.

I approach him slowly and try to put my hand on his back to guide him, but he swats me away.

Chapter Twenty

"Come on! We need to get out of this smoke!" I shout over the flames.

He drives his fist into my gut—I should've expected that—and darts through the back of the house.

Once I've recovered, I follow him but stop short as soon as I reach the threshold into the kitchen. The fire must've been started in here and the suspected arson's journey across the room was the floor's last straw. Sparks and flame sweep up toward my face as the support beams beneath give out and the floor caves in to the basement. Turning, I sprint out the front door and around to the back, determined to get the bastard who started these fires.

Over the wooden fences separating the yards, I see him jumping over the last one onto Second Street. I hop into the air once I'm surrounded in fire and rocket straight down to the arsonist. We collide hard and slam into the sidewalk. Lucky for me, he breaks most of my fall.

Scrambling on top of him, I manage to pin him down as a police car whizzes by to turn onto North Center Street where the fires are. Brakes squeal as they spot me and a moment later, an officer is running toward us.

"Chased him out of the third burning house," I tell him. "I think he started the fire."

"Is that so, Fire Boy?" he asks sarcastically.

"It's Heat," I correct. "And ask any of those witnesses on the lawn. I wasn't here until the fires were already lit."

The officer pushes me aside to put the arsonist in cuffs. "I'll be back to talk to *you*," he tells me as he leads the man off to his car.

"I'll be here—"

Beneath me, a portal opens and I'm sucked through into the street and away from the scene entirely.

Chapter Twenty-One

On the other side of the portal, I slam onto gravel. I barely register that I'm sliding along the side of a mountain before my momentum carries me down farther and farther in a dizzying somersault. My head bangs against rock. A mix of blood and dust coats my mouth. My skin aches with each fresh new bruise.

Suddenly, I'm not falling anymore. Instead, I'm rolling in tall grass. Finally, my body comes to a stop and I roll onto my back and stare up at the morning sky. My vision spins, but I know I don't have any time to lay here and hope that it stops. He's here.

The Gatekeeper.

My head's pounding and my chest heaves from the smoke at the fire, but still I force myself up onto wobbly legs. All I want to do is crumble on the ground, but I press on. I won't let them get the best of me.

Across the field I spot him. His dark trench coat blows lightly in the wind and the hood over his head conceals his face.

Chapter Twenty-One

Not that I'd be able to see it anyway. The image of the leather mask he wears is still burned into my mind.

The Gatekeeper steps in my direction and reaches for me, but fire ignites at my hands and I wave it toward him as a warning.

Instead, he points beneath my feet and I slip into a portal again, landing flat on my back on the ground right next to him. He reaches down and roughly grabs the front of my suit to pull me closer to his face. "Never hire someone to do a job if you want it done right."

He throws me back down but instead of hitting the ground, I slip into another orb, coming out face-first several feet above the ground this time.

My body is stiff and sore from the morning's events. By the time I roll onto my back, the Gatekeeper is at my side again, leaning closer to my face. "Although, the addition of powers does make this more interesting. I mean, I could drop you wherever I like."

I bring my arms up to latch onto him. If he's going to send me into another portal, I'm taking him with me.

My fingers just barely graze his trench coat as I sink into another orb. When I come out, I'm falling again. The air is momentarily sucked out of my lungs with the chill and my ears pop with the new altitude.

I'm high above the city, directly above the towers downtown. The wind rushes past me as I race back toward the earth. I'm higher than the mountain. Higher than most airplanes.

Faster and faster I drop toward the ground.

It takes me a few seconds, but I regain my breath, get my bearings, and spot the field we must've been in among an opening in the trees on the eastern mountain.

My body erupts in flames and I zoom in that direction. It's some of the last of my energy, but this could be my chance to finish him.

Another orb opens directly in front of me, leaving me no

time to dodge it. I manage to turn, but still I collide into the ground, creating a small crater where I land.

This is it. It's over. I have no more strength left in me. My vision fades in and out and I struggle to bring air into my chest after the impact. God only knows if I've broken anything.

All I can do is groan when I spot the Gatekeeper step into my line of sight.

"You're lucky I have more important business to deal with."

"ASH!" PERRY CALLS through the tall grass.

"Ash, please answer us!" Rachel adds.

I roll to my side and let out another groan. My body aches, but nothing hurts *too* bad. I don't think I've broken anything.

"Here!" I shout, lifting my hand up into the air. The strain becomes too much and I fall to the ground again.

The rustling of grass tells me they've heard me and a moment later, they're both beside me, pulling me to my feet.

"Are you okay?" Perry asks.

"We need to get him to the lab," Rachel says.

"I'm fine," I murmur. "Just tired. No breakfast and all."

"We'll get you something to eat," Perry says. "First, we need to get you down to the car. It's not that far."

By the time we reach Perry's car, I've realized that he's a liar. "Not that far" ended up taking us nearly half an hour. Of course, it was probably due to my short steps.

As he peels out of the parking lot at the base of the trail—the same one Vernon brought me to when he was showing me around the city—Rachel sits with me in the back seat and pulls off my mask.

"You're filthy," she says.

"But healthy, right?" I cough up some of the residual smoke from my throat. "Right now is not my finest hour, but

Chapter Twenty-One

I'm still not that bad."

"We need to get you out of this suit," she says.

"Rachel, what are you going to do right this moment?" Perry asks. "Just wait until we get to the lab. It's Sunday. Nobody will be there."

"At least have some water." Rachel tries to help me drink, but when Perry turns, it spills all down the front of me.

Finally, I grab the bottle from her and take a big sip, coughing more as the smoke coating my lungs is cleared away. Despite that, the water helps clear my head so I drink some more.

"Better?" she asks.

"Much. Any more?"

Rachel leans up to look in the cup holders by Perry.

"That was all I had," he tells her. "We'll be there soon anyway."

Twenty minutes later, I'm lying on the hospital bed in the medic room. Rachel's quiet as she monitors my vitals.

"I brought up all the ice packs I could find." Perry comes through the door with his arms full of cold compresses.

"Good, he's going to need them." Rachel hands them to me. "These are going to be really cold, but they'll help with any swelling."

Reluctantly, I pull back the warm blanket and place them on several areas of my body. After I took the suit off, all they had at the lab for me to wear was a hospital gown, which makes putting the ice packs on my worst bruises easier.

"Damn, that's cold!" I mutter. "When are you going to run back to your place to get me some clothes to wear?"

"I'll get there," Perry says. "For now, we need to talk about some things."

"First, tell me about the fire victims," I say. "Is everyone okay?"

"That was actually one of the things I wanted to tell you," he says. "They're all okay. Mrs. Hanson, the grandmother who was watching her grandson for the night, is in the hospital because of smoke inhalation. The news said her grandson would've been too if Heat hadn't wrapped him in a blanket first."

"That was all him," I say. "But that's good that everyone's okay."

"Yeah," Rachel chimes in. "And you're okay too, despite the blow to the head."

"That explains the drool," Perry jokes.

I shoot him a look.

"All your injuries appear to be superficial," she explains. "I mean, smacking your head like that resulted in a minor concussion, but for the most part your body is just bruised."

"Even though I essentially flew right into the ground?" I ask.

"I have a theory that because you were flying through the air, your body was pretty limp, meaning that you were able to withstand the impact better because you weren't tensed up."

I look over at Perry for a better explanation.

"You bounced."

I nod. "Interesting…and there were no harmful effects from that?"

"Well, you're bruised everywhere," she says.

"Oh, right." I turn back to Perry. "What else did you have to tell me?"

"We'll get to that," he says. "First, I want to know what happened. I mean, after you took off, I called Rachel to tell her what was going on. We watched the news at her place until one of the cops they interviewed said you disappeared in a portal."

"That's when we rushed down here so Perry could activate the tracer he put in your suit," she finishes.

"I wasn't aware that I was bugged, but I can't argue with the fact that it saved my life," I say.

"So what happened when you disappeared?" he asks.

"We went to the top of the mountain," I start. "The Gatekeeper said something about not hiring anyone to do his work. I'm going to guess he meant Vernon."

Chapter Twenty-One

"Why?" Rachel asks.

"Because he's the one who's been attacking me as Black Magnet," I say. "Not to mention, I'm sure it's not a coincidence that he's been going out of his way to try to get close to me."

She shakes her head. "I don't know. I still don't believe it. There has to be someone else."

"Rachel, we would've seen someone else by now," Perry argues.

"What about the bank robbery?" she asks. "That wasn't Black Magnet. And the fire? That wasn't him either. Maybe this is random too."

"They started *fires*, Rach," I say. "That's not a coincidence. I think it's pretty likely that they were hired by Vernon. I very much doubt that the Gatekeeper would contact people like that directly."

"How do you think Vernon and the Gatekeeper are connected?" Perry asks me.

"I think he hired Vernon, just like you guys said before. Or blackmailed him. Either way, Vernon is doing the Gatekeeper's dirty work."

He nods. "That's what I was thinking too. Did the Gatekeeper say what he wanted?"

"To kill me or hurt me or something," I say. "I think he might have something planned."

"Like what?" Rachel asks.

I shrug, then wince as my sore muscles stretch. "Ooo. I don't know. But it was pretty obvious he just wanted me out of the way."

"Do you think he's going to hurt Vernon?" she asks.

Perry shakes his head. "I don't think so. Ash couldn't have been the only reason the Gatekeeper hired him. And even so, if he wants to punish Vernon, he's going to hurt—or even just threaten—whatever leverage he has on him."

"What do you think that is?" I ask.

"Money?" Rachel offers.

"I can't imagine Vernon would put up with all of this for money," Perry says. "No, I think it might be his family. I hope I'm wrong, but I just have this feeling."

"That would make sense," she says. "He would do anything for his family."

"And the Gatekeeper—whoever *that* is—is exploiting that," I say. The more I think about it, the more it makes me mad. How can someone take advantage of someone else's love for their family?

Another thought hits me: "Do you think Vernon started those fires as a trap for me?"

Perry and Rachel exchange looks.

"We, uh, already considered that," she says quietly.

Perry points over to his computer in the next room. "I was listening in to the police scanner and they said witnesses saw a man fleeing the scene just before you disappeared in the portal."

"No, I know that," I say. "I fought him. The police arrested him. Besides, that little boy said he saw him too. But do you think Vernon hired that guy to start the fires to lure me out or do you think he just saw an opportunity and took it?"

"You fought him?" Perry asks.

"You really have had a rough morning," Rachel adds.

"Yeah, I guess so."

"So you think Vernon hired someone so that he wouldn't have to do as many bad things himself?" she asks. "Is that what you're trying to say?"

I shrug—and wince—again. "Yeah, I guess so. I mean, do you think deep down inside Vernon is still the friend you guys knew?"

"I certainly hope so." She takes a seat in a nearby chair and buries her face in her hands.

"I think that makes the most sense," Perry says. "But really, it doesn't matter. He's still trying to get rid of you because the

Chapter Twenty-One

Gatekeeper wants to get rid of you. And we don't know why."

"Story of my life," I murmur.

"Actually, we did clarify something about your past," Rachel says.

"You did?"

"Remember when we said that the high levels of heavy metals in the cave is what gave you your powers?" she asks.

I look to Perry again.

"The mercury and stuff."

"Oh, yeah. What about it?"

"We were completely overlooking the fact that the cave is only a cave because it was the entrance to the coal mine that runs through it," she explains. "The coal mine that experienced a serious explosion in the late sixties that killed a lot of people and shut down the plant. Actually, it nearly crippled the city's economy."

I scratch my forehead. "So what does that mean?"

"It means that not only were there harmful chemicals on the surface, but there might've been even more deeper inside the mine," Perry says. "So depending on where you traveled during your time in the cave, it might explain your memory loss and further explain your powers."

"But you said there wasn't anything extra in my blood?"

She shakes her head. "It's hard to tell what you were exposed to now, two weeks after you first woke up. We'd need a time machine or something to go back and follow you around."

I roll my eyes. "Or just my memory." I make fists with both hands and look up to the ceiling with a groan. "Ugh! I wish I could remember!"

Rachel grabs my wrists and steadies them. "It's okay, Ash. Look, besides today's attacks, you're perfectly healthy as far as I can tell. Whether or not you remember why you were in that cave and whether or not you were exposed to more dangerous substances, it really doesn't matter. You're here. You're healthy.

And you're doing what you can to help people. That's all you can do."

"It's more than you need to do, really," Perry adds.

She smiles at me. "But you're a good person, so you're going above and beyond."

I offer a half-hearted smile. "Thanks for trying to cheer me up, guys. I just really need to get some sleep now."

"Oh sure," she says. "Do you want to head home or just crash here?"

I yawn. "Here's fine."

Perry pats me on the shoulder. "I'll run home and get you some real clothes to wear while you're asleep. Rest up. Sounds like you're going to need it."

After they've left and turned out the light, my mind races with images from this morning: the families watching their homes burn, the boy hiding scared under his blankets, and the first thing the Gatekeeper said to me. *Never hire someone to do a job if you want it done right.*

Vernon's family is also on my mind. I might not have been the most comfortable at his house, but I was welcomed nonetheless. They're good people. They're his family. And rightfully, they're who he's choosing over me.

I wonder what that'll mean when push comes to shove.

Chapter Twenty-Two

"Dude, come on, you're not even ready!" Perry slings his bag over his shoulder in the kitchen and then pops a bagel between his teeth. "This is not the way to start the week," he says around his food.

It's the day after the whole fiasco with the Gatekeeper and I'm still not happy about how easily I was tricked. The couch—my makeshift bed—is where I plan to stay all day. I don't really know what I'm going to do, but right now I have a good stare going at the side of the neighboring brick building and that's holding my attention for the moment.

"I'm not going," I tell him.

"What do you mean?"

"I'm staying here."

He sighs and comes around the breakfast bar and takes a seat at one of the stools. "You're not feeling any better?"

A loaded question.

No, I'm not feeling better at all. Physically, my body is still bruised and exhausted from the Gatekeeper making me his bitch. Mentally, I'm wiped. Frustrated that even though I have all this power, I still wasn't able to stop them.

"No, I'm not," I finally say.

"Come on, Rachel can—"

"No, Perry."

Ever since I woke up in the cave, it's been go-go-go trying to figure out who I am and where I come from. I haven't really had a chance to breathe. I need a day to just relax. Above all else, I'm still human.

He clears his throat. "Does this have anything to do with us having to save you? Because we weren't trying to make you feel inferior. We were just worried about you."

I scoff. "That's not what it is."

"Okay," he says through a breath. "So is this about the fire—"

"Perry, I appreciate what you're trying to do, but I'm not going."

"All right, why don't you tell me what the problem is instead of leaving me to guess, huh?"

I don't say anything.

"Ash, come on," he pushes. "I might not have known you for that long, but I *do* know you. Spill."

"I just don't see the point of trying to figure out a way to go after the Gatekeeper when he's proven several times now that I'm no match for him."

"You'll get—"

"I said I'm not going, Perr."

Neither of us say anything. I keep my eyes locked on the imperfections of the brick wall outside the window. The discoloration of each piece, how it all blends together to make something remarkable.

Without a word, he gets up and heads to the door. He hesitates, but finally says, "We're only trying to help. It would be easier if you didn't shut us out." A moment later, I hear the door close and I'm left alone.

I lay where I am for a few minutes, still studying the bricks. Really I'm worrying that I'm hurting the relationships I have with the people who've been there for me from the beginning. Well, my beginning. My *new* beginning.

Tomorrow, I'll apologize. To both of them. I know Perry's right: they *are* only trying to help and it *would* be easier if I didn't make them the enemy. I need to grow up about it. Easier said than done.

When I can't stand my own thoughts anymore, I reach over and grab the remote from the coffee table and click on the news. I relish in the fact that I don't have to move from where I am on the couch.

A young beautiful blonde woman sits behind a desk in a blue dress. The camera pans out and to her right, a box appears and shows clips from the three houses that were destroyed yesterday morning. The next clip is a shaky video of me as Heat slipping into the orb that appeared on the pavement.

I turn up the volume.

"...Authorities say they have one man in custody who is accused of starting the fires. They believe he may have had other accomplices as well, however they're still at large."

The crisp, clear video cuts to a police officer on the street in front of the destroyed homes. He's a middle-aged man with thinning blond hair and his sunglasses pushed to the top of his head. Behind him, lights from a fire truck flash out of focus and other men in uniforms move around with purpose.

"We determined that the fires were all started in the kitchen of each house," he says. "I believe they intended for it to look like an accident, but three house fires in a row is no accident."

The clip cuts back to the blonde in the blue dress. "The man who calls himself Heat was reportedly spotted at the crime scene by a police officer. Authorities haven't commented on whether or not they believe he was involved in the arsons, but News 4 does have video of Heat stopping a bank robbery downtown on Saturday, saving at least ten hostages. He's also been credited with stopping a high-speed chase a couple weeks ago. Again, whether or not he was involved in these fires is yet to be determined, but the Ellsworth Police Department is asking anyone with information to step forward."

I change the channel. That didn't help my confidence at all. Do people really think I would set several houses on fire and then stop a high-speed chase? What kind of M.O. would that mean I have? Of course, I'm sure it was no accident that these people were ordered to start *fires*. Obviously, it'd be connected to me.

I settle on a sitcom marathon that holds my attention until my stomach growls with hunger. Clicking off the TV, I ease my way onto my feet, immediately feeling pain as my muscles are forced into action. The bruises up and down my body are still very present. I should ice the worst spots.

When I make it to the fridge, someone knocks on the door.

I freeze and stare at it. A brief, irrational fear waves over me: what if it's the Gatekeeper? Or one of the thugs that Vernon's been hiring?

Yeah, like any of them would knock.

"It's me, Ash," Rachel calls from the other side.

I let out the air I hadn't realized I'd been holding and open the door.

"Hey." It isn't until her eyes look me up and down that I realize I haven't quite gotten dressed yet. Most of the bruises are on full display. Luckily, I'm at least wearing shorts.

"I guess I didn't really believe it when Perry said you were bumming it today." She steps in and closes the door behind her.

"Yeah." I dig through the fridge for some luncheon meat to make a sandwich.

She takes a seat at the breakfast bar. "Anyway, I thought we should talk."

Chapter Twenty-Two

"About what?" I limp across the small kitchen to the opposite side of the counter Rachel's sitting at. Stiff legs from not moving at all this morning.

She points down. "Well, for one thing, have you even been icing at all? That bruise on your back is starting to turn colors."

"I will, yeah." I finish making my sandwich and hobble back over to the fridge again to put everything away.

"Let me do that," she says in an exasperated tone. "You go sit on the couch." She opens up the freezer and pulls out two ice packs. "Don't you have more?"

I shrug and feel the muscles in my back and shoulders stretch. I roll my shoulders a few times to loosen them up. "You'd have to ask Perry that."

"Hmm, well, just put these on then."

I grab everything and head back to the living room. Leaning back against one of the ice packs on the couch, I place the other one on my side across my ribs. My breath catches as the cold hits my bare skin.

When she joins me on the couch, I ask, "So what did you want to talk about?"

I know exactly what she wants to talk about—

"Do you have feelings for me?"

I nearly choke on my sandwich. Wasn't expecting that. "What?"

She takes a deep breath and dives into her story. "Evan seems to think that you do and we had this big fight last night, which started because Perry came over unannounced—which I get because it was about you, but I couldn't *tell* Evan it was about you, because the *you* we were discussing was Heat but from the way Evan saw it, I now have my male coworkers showing up at my house at all hours and he seems suspicious, but mostly suspicious of you because, let's face it, you just showed up out of the blue."

It all comes out in one long, exasperated breath and when

she's done I can't help but laugh, which brings attention to more bruises.

"Ash…" She looks at me through her eyebrows and then joins me in laughing. "Okay, I guess I did kind of unload on you. I'm sorry."

I shake my head. "No, it's okay. I get it. It does seem odd. But Rachel, you know why I've been coming over and stuff."

"Yeah, I get that part, but you seemed—I don't know—weird, when you found out I had a boyfriend." She shrugs. "I might just be reading into things."

I take another bite of my sandwich, not sure what to say.

She lets out a deep breath. "Look, I guess you don't really have to tell me—although not answering might be answer enough—but I just need you to be aware of how you're feeling so it doesn't affect our working relationship…or my personal one with Evan." She studies her nails. "I'm sorry if I ever led you on, but it's not like I've been hiding the fact that I have a boyfriend."

"I know."

Rachel hooks an eyebrow. "Then what was with all the questions the night of Vernon's party?"

I swallow another bite. "I don't know. I'm sorry too. I shouldn't have said anything about him. He's—you can do what you want. If he's important to you, I can't really stop you from spending time with him."

"Yeah."

We're quiet as I finish eating my sandwich. I didn't expect her to show up like this—or ask that question—although I probably should have anticipated that it was coming eventually. I can only play indifference for so long and clearly I wasn't that good at hiding it.

"So what's with the sick day?" she asks. "Perry says you were kind of discouraged this morning."

"Kind of? Try extremely."

She gives me a sad smile. "You'll get him, Ash. Both of them."

Chapter Twenty-Two

"Even if I do, what am I going to do afterward?" I wave to the TV. "People don't know what to make of me. And even the people who do think I'm helping, what are they going to say if I don't get the Gatekeeper or Black Magnet? The two guys that the police can't handle. And what if the people who hate me are right? It's not like I can remember whether I *am* a horrible person."

Rachel shakes her head. "You're not. If you were, it would've shown itself by now. You're good. But you're human. And if you're living your best life, you're likely to make a few enemies along the way."

"I guess so."

"I bet you did everything you could yesterday. I really believe you gave it your best shot." She looks off into the messy living room. "There's never a time when you don't."

"Well, minus right now."

She smiles. "True. You're not your best self right now, but that's okay. You need a break, which is understandable. Like I said, you're human."

I chew on my bottom lip and stare down at the messy coffee table, not a word between us.

After a moment, she asks, "What's the matter?"

"I'm afraid I won't be able to beat them," I admit. "I didn't have a chance to even get back on my feet before the Gatekeeper was throwing me through another portal. What happens if he kills me? Then who'll protect the city? And what if he *doesn't* kill me and just decides to torture me or something? I don't want—"

"Stop it," she says firmly. "That's not going to happen again. We're going to figure out who the Gatekeeper is and what makes his powers tick. He has to have gotten them from somewhere, just like you. If we can find a way to counteract that, then you'll be able to get him." She leans down to catch my eyes. "Perry and I aren't going anywhere. You can lean on us instead of wallowing in this messy apartment. Seriously, does he even own a vacuum?"

I laugh. "Thanks, Rach. For being there for me. For having faith in me. For everything."

"Of course. You've become a really great friend."

I smile. "What do you say I take a shower, put some real clothes on, and head back to ESTR with you so we can start working on a plan to stop the Gatekeeper *and* Black Magnet?"

She makes a face. "Actually…it's probably a good idea for Perry and I to have a day to completely focus on our *actual* jobs. You know, the stuff that pays our bills?"

I scrunch my face. "Sorry, I didn't think about that."

"It's okay. Besides, you should probably spend the day resting. Keep icing. Maybe take a cold shower or bath. It'll help the bruising. Take care of yourself for a day."

I nod. "You're probably right."

She points a finger at me as she gets up and heads to the door. "I *am* right. I'll check in with you later."

"Thanks again, Rach."

Chapter Twenty-Three

"Mr. Ash?" Mia says when she answers the door to the Michaels' house. "Come in, come in." She waves me through the door and I step inside.

"Thank you." I offer a polite smile.

"What brings you by?"

"Uh…I was hoping to talk to Mrs. Michaels, if she's available."

Her brow furrows in confusion, but still she nods and says, "I'll see if she's free. Why don't you take a seat in the parlor?"

She leads me to the room at the corner of the house, near the front door. After she leaves, I notice how quiet the house is. No sign of the kids home or anyone fussing in the kitchen. I wonder if the Michaels are even home, but then, Mia would've known that right away.

I haven't been back to this house since I snuck out the window during the dinner party. I wonder if Daniela was glad that I left. She never seemed to really take to me, but then, if my spouse had showed up one day with a random stranger to live with us indefinitely, I wouldn't be happy either.

My leg bounces nervously as I wait, my sneakers squeaking on the hardwood floor. The coffee table is glass, the couch isn't very comfortable, and the unlit candles in the candlesticks indicate that this room is only used for guests. Meanwhile, I'm technically homeless, bumming it on Perry's couch.

"Good evening, Mr. Ash," Daniela says in her slight accent as she steps into the room.

I stand to greet her and extend my hand, but she doesn't seem to notice it as she takes her seat, making sure her dress lays flat and her legs are tucked delicately to the side.

With as much dignity as I can muster, I retake my seat.

"What brings you in this evening?" she asks.

Looking down at my hands, I stammer, "Uh…"

For as much as I considered the different ways to initiate this conversation, I'm drawing a blank now that it's staring at me in the face.

"Is Vernon in?" I finally ask.

She frowns slightly. "I'm afraid he's not."

"Do you know when he will be back?"

"Is there something I can help you with?" she asks.

"I'm…worried about him," I say. "The last time I saw him we, uh, had a bit of an argument."

"When did you last see him?" Her eloquence slips away.

I study her, trying to determine if her concern is genuine or a cover story. My heart goes out to her, though. This isn't a woman covering for her husband, it's a woman *concerned* about her husband.

"This past weekend," I tell her. "He…didn't look good."

Daniela brings a hand to her mouth. Her proper persona quickly fading away.

"Are you saying *you* haven't seen him?" I ask.

She squeezes her eyes shut tight and shakes her head ever so slightly.

Chapter Twenty-Three

"Oh. As far as I knew, Vernon's been coming home every night," I say. "I take it that's not the case?"

She sucks in her bottom lip and turns away, blinking her eyes hard. "No, he hasn't been home in some time."

"How long?" I ask.

"A week or so," she responds. "Where do you think he is? Is he having an affair? Doing drugs? Kidnapped?"

"I don't know," I say with a shrug. "Was he acting any differently at all before he stopped coming home?"

"Well, that was right after you…"

Right. Just after I arrived and intruded on their family.

"What changed?" I ask.

"He started coming home later, sometimes not at all. But I always knew where he was until…I didn't."

"Did he call you to tell you where he was?" I ask.

She shakes her head. "Texts, mostly. There were only a few phone calls. But the last time I talked to him was two days ago and I don't want to overreact and call the police but I'm just not sure—" She brings a fist to her mouth again as she's overcome with emotion. She dabs at her eyes, but a moment later she lets out a loud sigh. "I have no idea where my husband is."

"What were his reasons for being gone?" I ask. "Where did he say he was going? Who was he with?"

She pulls a tissue out of the box sitting on the glass coffee table and wipes away her runny makeup. "He said he was working late. He's *always* working late."

"So he was at the office?" I push.

"That's what he told me, but I don't see how he could be gone for that long." Daniela looks out of the room toward the front door. "He always tells me where he is. *Always*."

I don't say anything for a moment while she tries to regain her composure. I can't imagine the pain she's going through. It's likely the same pain my family is going through—wherever they are. Clearly, the neighborhood I thought was mine wasn't mine.

Just like where Daniela thought her husband was going wasn't *actually* where he was.

"Did he say who he was working with at the office?" There's a small part of me that hopes—despite all the evidence against him—that I've made the wrong assumption about Vernon and he's not actually Black Magnet.

She tosses up her hands. "I don't know! It's always, 'Mr. Cain needs this. Mr. Cain needs that.' It's like he's married to Mr. Cain rather than me!"

"Mr. Cain?"

"Yes, Arlus Cain," she says. "I believe you met him when we hosted Vernon's last dinner party."

Right. The guy I met right before getting that weird vision. The one Perry and I needed to escape from out the bathroom window.

"Right, right." I nod slowly, pacing myself before launching into my next several questions. "What else has your husband said about Mr. Cain?"

Her demeanor noticeably changes, likely sensing the shift in my questions from worried and curious to invasive and suggestive.

"Not much. Whenever he talks about him, it's always business stuff. I don't really pay attention to the details."

"But you suspect he could be with Mr. Cain now, correct?"

"I'm not sure. It's possible."

I wonder how much my friends at ESTR know about Vernon's and Arlus's relationship. They kind of ruled Arlus out of any suspicious behavior because of his age, but that doesn't mean anything. If Vernon is Black Magnet—and I'm becoming more and more convinced that he is—then it seems as though Arlus Cain is somehow involved.

"What do you know about Arlus?" I ask.

She shrugs. "Not much, really. My husband only talks about him in the context of work."

Chapter Twenty-Three

"But he must have some sort of personal relationship with him," I say. "He had him here for that dinner party and seemed eager to introduce me to him."

Daniela meets my eyes. "If you're insinuating Mr. Cain has ill-intentions, I'd have to dis—"

I interrupt. "Did Vernon ever talk about Arlus before I came to stay with you guys for that week?"

She considers this. "Not as much, no."

I rise to my feet. "Okay. Thank you, Mrs. Michaels. I'll keep my eye out in case I hear anything about your husband."

"Actually, Mr.…Ash, I have a question for you." She stands as well to meet my eyes. "I don't believe I ever caught your last name."

I smile at her as I consider my response. The longer it takes, though, the more her distrust for me grows.

"Mrs. Michaels," I finally say, "I am not the enemy here. Please don't take the doubt you're developing in your husband out on the people who are only trying to help you. That kind of thinking only stands to alienate yourself from those you need most."

She returns my smile, which is now only a thin veil masking our true feelings toward one another. "With all due respect, Mr. *Ash*, I am very well aware of the importance of support systems, however, I would also like to remind you that a marriage is between two people and those two people only."

"Thank you for your time, Mrs. Michaels."

She walks me to the door and doesn't offer anything else to me as I step out and she promptly shuts—and locks—the door behind me.

Following the brick path back to the sidewalk, I consider what the consequences might be for overstepping with Vernon's wife. Except, whatever wrath that's coming my way will not be because of a conversation I had with Daniela. Black Magnet is coming for me and if he really has been studying his opponent, he would've already anticipated this conversation.

I turn right to head north through downtown back to Perry's apartment. It's just after five. He should be home soon. I'll have to tell him about my visit to the Michaels. If he's not mad at me for going alone, maybe he can help me look into Arlus Cain more. He's definitely a person of interest.

Just before I reach the lights of downtown, I pass under thick tree cover that casts the sidewalk into shadow. The setting sun shines in my eyes and I fail to see the orb open up on the sidewalk in front of me. The next step I take, I slip inside and disappear.

Chapter Twenty-Four

On the other side of the portal, I collapse on the floor at ESTR. Expecting to be immediately grabbed and restrained, I'm surprised when all I hear is the air blowing through the vents.

Strange…

Slowly, I rise to my feet and spot my Heat suit in the medic room. I forgot to grab it yesterday after the fires. Quickly, I pull it on. The Gatekeeper brought me here for a reason. I'm going to need all the help I can get.

As I step out of the medic room, I hear the clanging metal of Black Magnet's suit. Slinking against the wall, I try to sneak up on him, but the next moment Vernon's nearly in my face. Both of us are momentarily startled, but ultimately he's the one who makes the first move, swinging his arm back and sending Perry's metal work table flying at me, pinning me against the wall by magnetism.

Vernon stands before me, dressed as Black Magnet with the

exception of the helmet. All my hopeful doubts of him *not* actually being one of my enemies is now completely out the window.

"Vernon," I start once I've regained the air in my lungs.

"Ash." He looks at me solemnly.

"Your wife is quite worried about you. You should probably give her a call."

He charges toward me and pounds the wall right beside my face. I force myself to keep my eyes locked with his and not flinch.

"What have you done with her!?" he bellows.

I roll my eyes. "Relax. Unlike you, I've been straightforward from the start. *I* haven't killed anyone or done harm to anyone for no reason."

His eyes bore into me.

"She's fine," I tell him. "We just had a chat. I was wondering where you were and what she knew. Seems like you left her in the dark. It's probably a good thing, too. But then, the Gatekeeper might still kill her. Where is he, by the way? Is he lurking in the hallway?"

He grunts and backs away from me. "No. He's not here."

"Well then, he dropped me off to you so I'm going to say that he's trying to tell you something."

Vernon turns away from me and sits at Rachel's desk. "I know, I know, I know. Do you have any idea how *infuriating* you are? I've been trying for *two weeks* to get answers about you, making every attempt to get in here and find *something*!"

"Answers about what?"

"Nothing! It doesn't matter." He opens up drawers, rifles through papers, and finally turns to her computer.

"What are you looking for?"

"Rachel's research," he says.

"On me?"

Chapter Twenty-Four

He types in a password. Just over his shoulder, I see a red X pop up. Wrong.

"Vernon!"

He ignores me. Again and again he tries various passwords to no avail. He shouts and pounds his fist on the desk. I've never seen him this angry. He snaps around to me. "Do *you* know the password?"

"Vernon, what's going on?"

After a few deep breaths, he seems to settle a little. "Sorry. I'm sorry. You're not the problem. This is just—it's too much! I can't—there's too much—he's going to hurt them."

"Hurt who?" My mind flashes to any number of people who might be a victim due to Vernon's inability to obey the Gatekeeper's requests. His family. His coworkers. Rachel. Perry.

He cradles his head with his hands and stares at the floor a minute. I consider asking him more, but finally he speaks up.

"I'm sorry for attacking you as Black Magnet."

Well, there's a twist.

"Then why'd you do it?" I ask.

"He would've taken everything from me—he's probably going to."

"How? Are you afraid he's going to hurt you or your family?"

Vernon scoffs and picks up his head, looking me in the eyes once again. "I've been paying his dues for *years*. Slowly escalating more and more. Now look at me. I'm a mutant who targets people I would otherwise consider my friend."

I do my best to soften my look. "I am your friend, Vernon. Tell me what's going on and maybe I can help you. Rachel and Perry could—"

"Rachel and Perry don't have the strength to do what needs to be done," he interjects. "Evidently, neither do you."

There's a slap in the face.

"I'm stuck."

"Why?"

He runs his tongue under his lip as he studies me. "Fifteen years ago, I didn't have any of this. I was newly married. I didn't work at River Valley Holdings. I didn't even *know* Arlus Cain."

"Arlus Cain? Your boss?"

Vernon smirks. "Yes, or as you've been calling him, the Gatekeeper."

I recount the dinner party at Vernon's. The vision that Arlus triggered. The way he tried to get through the door when Perry and I went up to my room. The way Vernon kept him at bay long enough for us to escape. Vernon's a good guy, despite what's he's done. Arlus, apparently, is not.

My shock must show, because Vernon nods with a grin. "There's a lot about Mr. Cain that you don't know."

"I guess so..."

"So fifteen years ago on New Year's Eve—or rather, this would've been very early in the morning on New Year's Day—my life changed completely. I had been at a party celebrating the New Year. Daniela had been working long hours, taking the holidays shifts. Yes, Ash, she used to work. She was a nurse at Ellsworth General Hospital.

"Anyway, she wasn't at the party, opting instead to get a good night's sleep. That left me to drive myself home. As it turns out, that was the worst mistake I could ever make.

"Before I left, I didn't feel like scraping off the ice from my windshield, so my field of view wasn't that good as I was driving. That's not to mention the fact that I had been drinking. I thought I had things under control—and I might have—but the fact that I couldn't see that well out of my windshield didn't help any."

He pauses and stares at the floor again.

"I didn't see her until she was right in front of me. By then it was too late. Even when I did hit the brakes, I slide on the ice. When I got out to look, half of her body was crushed underneath. The other half still clung to the hood of my car."

I swallow hard, picturing the scene in my head, but also wondering what this has to do with Arlus.

"It was Arlus's daughter," he says, as if reading my thoughts. "He showed up not long after the police and ambulance did. Obviously, he was completely heartbroken, but he was also pissed. By then, it had finally hit me what just happened—what I did to her and to her family. She couldn't have been older than twenty. One of the things they found in her bag was her college ID tag. She was going to be a social worker."

He closes his eyes and shakes his head. The memory obviously still haunts him.

"Arlus saw how upset I was. He realized it was an accident, but it still didn't bring his daughter back. So he pulled me aside and told me that he *should* sue me for everything I've got—which wasn't much at that point. Instead, he told me that if I went work for him—did everything he asked—that it would all go away."

I narrow my eyes, suspicious of this part of the story. It doesn't make sense. Why would a grieving father give his daughter's killer a job? What could Vernon have possibly done to make losing his daughter okay?

"Naturally, I agreed right away," Vernon goes on. "By the end of the week, I was released from jail. The police stopped calling. My court date was repeatedly pushed back until finally they just didn't give me a new one. I was free of it."

"But not really," I say. "It's fifteen years later and look where you are."

He nods. "Cain came to my door about a month after the accident and told me that one-by-one he had 'taken care of' most of the people who knew about what happened. All that was left were the wives, and I assured him right away that Daniela wouldn't talk about it unless she was prompted. But at that point, I thought that he had killed everyone who knew. Now I realize that he just transported them somewhere else. Maybe he killed them, I don't know. Maybe he dropped them in the middle of the ocean and left them to drown. Maybe he took them to the center of Antarctica and let nature takes its course. Again, I don't know. And honestly, I was so relieved at the time that my life wasn't over that I was willing to do anything the man asked. And he did."

"Your job?"

"Yes," he says with another nod. "He offered to train me at River Valley. It was a tiny start-up at the time. I figured he was just desperate for employees. The pay wasn't great and we worked out of a cramped basement office at first, but over the years it has grown tremendously. With each new growth, Mr. Cain made sure to keep me right by his side, which meant that I was financially compensated. But every time I went into his office, I saw the picture of his daughter on his desk and knew that all of my fortune was because of a tragic event."

"I'm sure Arlus reminded you of that again and again."

"Oh yeah. Especially in the last few weeks when you first turned up. See, you changed everything, Ash."

"Me? How?"

"You're the one Arlus had been expecting. And he didn't seem surprised by your abilities. In fact, that's when he told me about his...and gave me mine."

"He *gave* you yours? How?"

"The same way you got yours," he explains. "He called me into his office not long after the fire rain storm and told me he needed me to make good on my commitment to him once again. He opened a portal and told me to walk through—promising that I'd come out with extraordinary abilities like him or you. But told me I needed to keep it secret.

"When I stepped through the portal it was completely dark. I had no idea where I was or how to get out. The odor in the air is what struck me at first. I couldn't place it, but I knew it wasn't safe. For twelve hours I was locked in there until finally, I was dropped through another portal and back into Cain's office. He told me that he needed me to kill you…or he'd kill my family."

Guess Rachel was right about his motivation.

"But Vernon, we can stop him," I plead. "Especially now that we know you have powers too. Together we can—"

"You don't think I haven't thought of that? Of course I have! But he has his own powers. And each time I see how he faces off against you, I'm reminded of just how powerful he is. The difference is, I have something at stake that I can't afford to lose. You, however, have *nothing* to lose."

"Then what's your plan?" I ask. "How are you going to get out from under his thumb?"

"With you," he says. "If I can find the research Rachel and Perry have already done on you, I can sell it—and you—to someone who's willing to pay me enough for me to pay off Cain and move my family away from here. Somewhere where we'll be safe."

"Vernon, it's not going to be that easy. Not anymore. You know too much. He's not going to let a liability like you escape simply because you give him money. He *has* money!"

"It's all I've got!" he bellows. "I have no other choice. I'm sorry, Ash."

"Then if you're going to take off, you need to tell me as much as you can about Arlus."

He studies me and lets out a deep breath. "What do you want to know?"

"Uh…" I didn't think it'd be that easy to convince him. "Well, first off, does he know who I am? Who I *really* am? Before I woke up in the cave."

Slowly, he nods. "He knows."

"Do you?"

"Not...not really. Sort of. I don't know if I believe it."

"Vernon, you have to tell me! We haven't come up with *anything*!"

"He claims that he's—it's impossible. He's gotta be...fifty years older than you!"

"What is it?"

"He says that he's your younger brother."

I definitely was not expecting that. Vernon's right. It's impossible. Arlus is an old man and the best we can figure out, I'm only about twenty, give or take a few years. But it would explain how the Gatekeeper knew my name the first time I faced off against him.

The door bursts open and Rachel charges through with a metal chair raised above her head, charging right for Vernon. She nearly hits him with it too, but he reacts before it can make contact and uses his magnetic force to send it flying away.

But the use of his powers against her chair, frees the magnetic hold on the desk pinning me to the wall. It crashes to the floor and I race toward Rachel in case anything is thrown her way. I don't think Vernon would intentionally hurt her, but he's desperate.

We dart into the hall and around the corner by the main doors.

"How did you know I was here?" I ask.

"Perry said you weren't home and I thought maybe you came back here to brainstorm some idea," she says.

"Where's Perry, then?"

"Parking the car, he'll be here any minute."

"No, you both need to get out of here," I tell her. "I'll distract Vernon."

"And what if he traps you again?"

"How are you going to stop him?"

"I just did, didn't I?"

Chapter Twenty-Four

Behind Rachel, an orb appears and before I even have a chance to process what's happening, the Gatekeeper—Arlus Cain, my brother—is standing right beside us.

Chapter Twenty-Five

Quickly, I grab Rachel and pull her away, back toward Lab #8. Just as we approach the door to the lab, Perry walks up from the back entrance.

"You're okay!" he tells me. "Why are you in your Heat suit?"

"No time to talk, we have to go." I grab his arm and try to lead him away, but he pulls back, waiting for an explanation.

"Perry, come on!" Rachel urges.

It's too late. The Gatekeeper is now right behind us again.

Pushing my friends behind me, I face him directly.

"Vernon!" I call out. "We could use a little help here!"

He joins us in the hallway and recoils when he sees his boss.

"I sent you him alone so you could take care of him," the Gatekeeper tells him. "Not to call the rest of them!"

"I didn't—I had him restrained, I promise you. He—he got away!"

"You can't control him anymore," I say. "It's over, Arlus. I know you're my brother."

Chapter Twenty-Five

"Brother?" Perry mutters.

My words send Arlus into a rage. He grabs Vernon by the metal plate protecting his front and slams him against the wall.

"Hey!" Perry barks from behind me.

"So you told him, huh?" the Gatekeeper snarls. "What about the unspeakable things you've done?"

"I know it all," I say.

"Yeah, just let him go," Rachel adds.

"Guys, get out of here," I tell them, keeping my eyes on the Gatekeeper.

"No, we're not leaving you," she says.

"I can handle it, just go!"

"You can handle it?" Arlus asks me. "Just like you've handled things before. Tell me, are you going to let these friends die like you've done in the past?"

Having no idea what he's talking about, I decide to make my move instead. Leaping at him, I try to break his hold on Vernon. Arlus stumbles back and Vernon hunches over and grasps at his throat, coughing.

"Are you okay?" I ask him.

Portals open all around us and fire streams through, just like it was the night after I woke up in the cave. Within a matter of seconds, the walls have caught fire, spreading to the rest of the building.

Wheeling around, I throw both hands in the Gatekeeper's direction and hurl a large fireball at his stomach that sends him flying back into the lab.

"Okay, I'm out of here!" Perry says.

I wave away the smoke in my face and point to the emergency exit not far down the hall. "Go!"

"No, we need to make sure the building's clear!" Rachel says. "Just make sure he doesn't start anymore fires. We'll be quick!" She grabs Perry and races down the hall toward the staircase that leads to the upper floors. I watch them leave until they're out of sight.

When I turn around, Arlus has Vernon by the throat, lifting him up into the air.

"Let him go!"

Instead, Arlus brings him closer to his chest, wrapping a second arm around him in a way that's almost like a headlock. In one quick move, I hear Vernon's neck snap and the life fade from his eyes. The metal clinging to Vernon's body falls with loud clangs.

Arlus drops Vernon to the floor and steps toward me.

Seeing his lifeless body thrown away like garbage sparks memories. I think about his wife, worried about where he is; his children, who will have to say goodbye to him too soon; his friends; his *life*. Ripped away because he no longer wanted to be manipulated.

"Brave friends you have," Arlus tells me.

"You killed him!" My fists ignite, just as the flames in the next room carry to the papers that Vernon threw across the room in his desperation. I ignore it, though. Arlus is the enemy now. Always was, really.

"You want me, right?" I say to him. "Well, here I am. Do what you want to me, but leave everyone else alone."

He chuckles. "You're no longer the older one. So naïve."

I narrow my eyes.

"My intention wasn't ever to hurt you physically, Ash. I just wanted to put you in your place. I let you establish roots here, make friends, retrace some semblance of your memory—that way it'll hurt more when I rip each and every thing you hold dear away from you, one by one."

I look down at Vernon. "But he was your ally."

"Yes, but since he turned on me, I have no use for him."

"So you *killed* him?" More anger bubbles in me and I hurl fireballs, one after the other, in Arlus's direction. Waving his hand in front of him, he creates a large portal that sucks up each of my fireballs.

Realizing it's not doing anything, I stop, more frustrated than ever.

"So impulsive," he says. "You always liked to talk with your fists."

I motion to Vernon, trying to keep my voice from wavering. "Like you're any different?"

"My anger is a tool I choose to use when it suits me," he says. "But I assure you, the only hatred I harbor is geared toward you alone."

"But why do you hate me?"

The sound of crashing from the next room breaks our conversation. The fire is taking its toll on the building. Within seconds, I see flames lick the doorway into the hall. I hope Rachel and Perry have already escaped.

"You know, the public still isn't sure what to make of you," Arlus says. "From the fire storms to the factory fire to the house fires to this, it appears as though along your path to help the city, you're simultaneously destroying it. I believe the flames you fire will soon consume you."

An orb opens behind him and he steps back into it.

My body bursts into flames and I dive right at him, wrapping my arms around his waist. Together, we sail straight into the portal.

On the other side, we come out on the roof of a building. I'm too focused on him and what happened at ESTR to notice where we've been transported to.

Arlus scrambles backward and pats out the flames on his long coat. Still on fire, I dive on top of him. Straddling him, I bring my hands to his neck, squeezing just the same way he did to Vernon.

Just like him.

Suddenly, I let go. This is not who I am.

The momentary break gives Arlus an opportunity to

deliver a kick to my chest. I'm hurled across the roof, rolling to the edge. The flames surrounding me dissipate and I'm left lying on the edge of the building.

Arlus walks over and presses his foot against my stomach. "I could end this right here. Forty stories up. One push is all it'll take."

"So do it," I mutter as weakly as I can. My body aches, both from him kicking me and the beating he gave me yesterday morning.

"This is it, brother," he says. "This is the end of the road for us."

"I'm sure you've said that before." I grab ahold of his leg.

He leaps backward, pushing his other leg out toward me on his way back, trying to push me off.

I hold tight, pulling us both over the edge, only letting go once we're free falling. I burst into flames again, this time soaring high into the sky and away from Arlus's falling body. I hover above the city and look out to get my bearings. We're downtown on the tallest tower in the city. The Fenty Building, I think is what Vernon called it. The lights twinkle below within the valley, but on the edge near the dreaded western mountain is an inferno.

The fire at the lab.

I need to get back to it to make sure Rachel and Perry and everyone else have gotten out okay, but I'm not sure if Arlus is still a threat. I need to make sure he's truly dead.

Reluctantly, I pull my eyes away from the burning lab and swoop down to the street. No sign of Arlus, but I can't afford to search too long. I need to get everyone to safety.

Zooming back into the sky, I take off in the direction of ESTR, only slowing once I've reached it. I land hard on the ground, my sore legs aching from the sudden impact, but there's no time to stop. I run inside, grateful for my mask because the smoke is so thick I can barely see anything.

Chapter Twenty-Five

Placing my hand on the wall, I follow it down to the entry of Lab #8, where Vernon's body lies. My eyes water from the smoke and I drop to my hands and knees beneath it. The air is clearer down near the floor.

For half a second, I consider leaving him here and hope they determine that the fire is what killed him. But no. That wouldn't be right. Keeping my head down low, I crawl to Vernon's body. I need to get him out of here. For his family, who he died trying to protect.

"Ash!" Rachel calls from down the hall.

"I'm okay!" I shout back to her.

"We need to get out of here!" Perry's voice grows louder as they approach. When they come into view, I see they've made make-shift masks out of cloth they've soiled in order to filter the air. They each hold it to their mouths, but still they're covered in soot.

"Everyone's out," he says. "There were only a few custodial workers left.

"Ash, the building is going to come down." Rachel breaks into a coughing fit before returning the cloth to her mouth.

"Help me get him out," I say.

Hooking my hands under his armpits, Rachel and Perry each grab his feet and together we carry him toward the emergency exit I pointed to earlier. When the door swings open, the flames surge forward with newfound strength and I stumble backward outside. Luckily, the door swings closed on its own, locking the flames in.

"Just a few more feet," I tell them. "Get him across the parking lot. That'll be enough."

The air out here is fresher, cleaner. With the various plastics and chemicals that are in the lab, there was no telling what kind of harmful substances Rachel and Perry were breathing in.

Out here, though, I can feel myself regain strength the

longer I breathe in this good air, even with the mask. Sucking in another good breath, I regain a bit more energy and we're able to haul him out to the sidewalk.

The effort depletes my energy. My body gives out and I collapse on the ground, as do Rachel and Perry.

"We did it," she says triumphantly.

Looking back at ESTR, though, I see the flames creeping out of the few windows in the building. It doesn't feel like a success, yet I know I got as many people out safely as I could. Reassuringly, I hear the sound of fire trucks roar in the distance.

Chapter Twenty-Six

Everyone wears black. The bright sun shining down on the cemetery contrasts the sad morning. Even though the service has ended, Daniela is still seated in the front row, right by Vernon's grave. She's inconsolable. Their children sit on either side of her, both looking grim. There's an ever-present lump in my throat as I imagine their future without Vernon.

I follow Rachel and Perry back to the car in silence. We're quiet even as we wait in the line of cars to exit the cemetery. It isn't until we're on the road that Perry speaks up.

"I'll miss him." His eyes don't waver from in front of him.

Rachel nods from the front seat. "Me too."

"I feel bad for his family," I say.

"Yeah," he says. "They'll get through it, though."

"Of course they will," she says. "It's just going to be tough."

"I feel like I should do something or say something—"

"Ash, don't," Rachel cuts me off. "This wasn't your fault.

You said the Gatekeeper killed him. And it was *his* fault the lab burned down."

"But shouldn't I have anticipated that?" I ask.

Perry shrugs. "Maybe, but you didn't. You had so much thrown at you at once. And there's no going back now. There's no way you'll ever be able to anticipate *everything*."

"I just wish my mistake hadn't killed someone."

"Of course." Rachel reaches back and touches my knee.

I squeeze her hand.

"Ash, you did the best you could," she says.

I don't say anything. I release her hand and she turns back to face the front.

We're quiet again. Perry takes the exit near his apartment. We never discussed what we were doing after the funeral. All three of us silently agreed that we didn't want to go to the reception. Watching Vernon's family grieve anymore and—heaven forbid—*talk* to them; none of us would've been able to handle that. It's selfish and cowardly, but I couldn't honestly look any of them in the face and pretend that I didn't know what happened.

"Do you think he got away?" I murmur.

"The Gatekeeper?" Rachel asks.

"Arlus Cain," Perry corrects.

"My brother."

"Are we sure it's true?" she asks. "You guys are…fifty years apart."

"It's impossible," Perry adds.

"So is shooting fire out of your hands," I counter.

He nods.

"Anyway, it's why he killed Vernon," I say. "I'm sure it's true."

"Somehow," he murmurs.

Ash Cain. The name doesn't ring a bell with me, but maybe it's because since I've woken up, I only ever associated *Cain* with someone who gave me a bad feeling—with good reason, apparently.

I shake my head. "I know it doesn't make sense, but now that I know he's my brother, I can almost picture him in those flashbacks I had where I was fighting the boy, you know? We were just kids then."

"Now that you have a face to put with the name, it makes sense that you're making those connections," Rachel says.

"Yeah."

She offers me a sad smile before changing the subject again. "So what's the likelihood that Arlus escaped?"

Perry turns into the parking lot for his apartment building. "Pretty good, I'd say."

"Why's that?" she asks.

"Can't be sure until we see a body."

"That's morbid," she says.

"It's what I was looking for after we fell," I tell them. "Before I flew back to the lab."

"And?" He pulls into a parking spot and shifts into park.

"Nothing. Either he opened another portal in midair and disappeared or his body landed somewhere that I couldn't see."

"So what do we do now?" Rachel asks.

Perry unhooks his seatbelt. "Well, it's not like he outed himself as the Gatekeeper to everyone. Just us. And that wasn't even him, it was Vernon."

"Most people probably don't even know about him," I add. "The Gatekeeper never really made public appearances."

None of us move to get out of the hot car. Too wrapped up in our conversation and the emotions from this morning.

"So let's change that," she suggests. "Bring the Gatekeeper into the papers to help bring up Heat's name."

"Oh, you're on board with the Heat name now?" Perry asks.

"It's grown on me," she says with the first smirk any of us

have had all day. "Besides, it'll come in handy. There might even be an investigation now that our lab's gone. Perry and I are both out of a job."

I never thought of that. Not only did ESTR catch fire, but Vernon died, who was their rep from River Valley Holdings, where Arlus Cain is the CEO. Their careers would be better off if Arlus *did* die.

"Now that Arlus's death is uncertain—" I start.

"*Unlikely* is more probable," Perry interjects.

"You guys should probably distance yourselves from River Valley Holdings," I finish.

"Well, don't go full drama queen on me yet," Perry says. "We'll figure it out."

"Yeah, I guess so." Rachel plays with her nails. She lets out a breath and turns to me. "What are we going to do if Arlus *did* survive?"

"We should continue under the assumption that he's alive until we know for sure," Perry adds.

"I don't know," I admit. "But I know one thing's true."

"What's that?" he asks.

"I need to regain my memories. I have work to do."

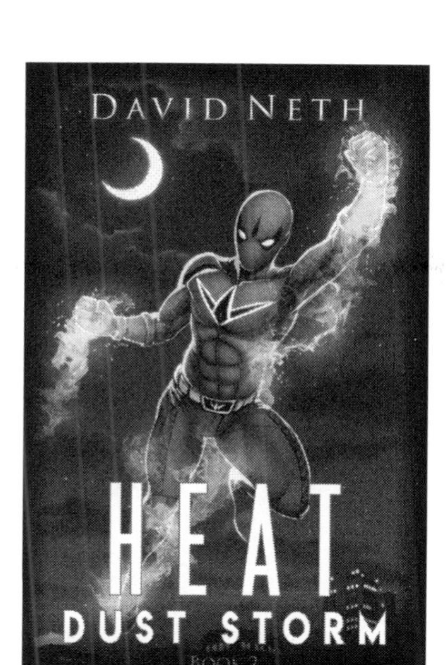

In the aftermath of Black Magnet's demise, Ash and his friends are still adjusting to the ramifications its had on their lives. Now equipped with a glimpse of who he was before he woke up in the mine, Ash is reluctant to learn more about himself and looks for anything to keep his mind off of his past.

When a student at Perry's new job at a nearby university winds up dead with no sign of attack other than sand scattered around the body, Ash finds the perfect distraction. Only, he can barely get answers on the first victim before another student is killed in the same way somewhere else on campus.

While attempting to solve the murders that Ash knows was done by a super, he soon finds himself in the cross-hairs of the police detective leading the investigation. In order to stop the super truly responsible for the murders, Ash is faced with a choice: take the fall for the attacks or expose himself as Heat.

More by the Author

To find the rest of the author's books visit
DavidNethBooks.com/Books

Subscribe to his newsletter to be the first to know of new releases and special deals!
DavidNethBooks.com/Newsletter

If you enjoyed the book, please consider leaving a review on Goodreads or the retailer you bought it from. Reviews help potential readers determine whether they'll enjoy a book, so any comments on what you thought of the story would be very helpful!

About the Author

David Neth is the author of the Heat series, Fuse series, the Under the Moon series, and other stories. He lives in Batavia, NY, where he dreams of a successful publishing career and opening his own bookstore.

Follow the author at

www.DavidNethBooks.com
www.facebook.com/DavidNethBooks
www.instagram.com/dneth13

Made in the USA
Columbia, SC
28 December 2019

85907348R00138